William Jo

Scapegrace at Sea

Vol. II

SALZWASSER
VERLAG

William Johnstoun N. Neale

Scapegrace at Sea

Vol. II

Reprint of the original, first published in 1863.

1st Edition 2022 | ISBN: 978-3-37500-180-3

Verlag (Publisher): Salzwasser Verlag GmbH, Zeilweg 44, 60439 Frankfurt, Deutschland
Vertretungsberechtigt (Authorized to represent): E. Roepke, Zeilweg 44, 60439 Frankfurt, Deutschland
Druck (Print): Books on Demand GmbH, In de Tarpen 42, 22848 Norderstedt, Deutschland

SCAPEGRACE AT SEA;

OR.

SOLDIERS AFLOAT AND SAILORS ASHORE.

IN THREE VOLUMES

VOL. II.

[SECOND EDITION.]

London:

1863.

SCAPEGRACE AT SEA.

CHAPTER I.

"Now, Julius, my boy," said his brother, "the first thing to-morrow morning you must go off to town and trace that note for me."

"I will do anything you tell me, but I know as much about tracing a note as I do about pruning a vine."

"Well, I will give you a note of introduction to my bankers, and as to the difficulty of tracing it, I do not suppose it requires anything more than merely to go to our bankers, and see one of the partners; tell him in confidence what has happened, and ask him to find out where it has been sent from."

"The only thing that militates against that proceeding is, that if you entrust me with the £500 note, the chances are nine hundred to one that I shall lose it before I get to the bank. I hate money. Is there no other mode of going to work?"

"Yes, I can do this. I can give you the number, and the date, and all particulars of it; in fact I will make a copy of it on a sheet of note paper."

"Ah! do, that is a good fellow, to-morrow morning before I go up. I shall be certain not to lose the copy, but I know my very anxiety about the original would end in my getting rid of it in some troublesome way or another."

On the following morning, Montagu made a complete copy of the note, and Julius took it off to town.

On going to the bankers, and asking to see one of the partners, a staid old gentleman, full of years and honor, with a few grey hairs still left about his head, received him very courteously in the bank parlour.

"I am afraid, sir," said the banker, "that this is a matter in which we cannot interfere. You see, sir, the note is a good note, and our only mode of proceeding would be to take it to the Bank of England and there use our private acquaintance with one of the officers of the bank, to find out to what private bank this was issued. Perhaps they might not feel at liberty to give us that information, and supposing they did, we should then have to proceed to the private bank indicated, and ask them to disclose to us to which of their customers this £500 note was issued.

"Precisely," said the young sailor, "you get that information, and that is all we want."

"Yes, my dear sir, but," said the banker,

bowing very politely, "what do you suppose any customers of ours would say if we revealed to you any of their private transactions with us? Suppose, my dear sir, any one came to us and asked us to tell them what was the amount of your balance in our hands, or in what shape, or in what quarter you draw it, what would you say to us if we broke our confidence with you, and disclosed it?"

"I do not suppose I should say much, because I should not care myself if my account was published at Charing Cross; but I daresay there are some fidgety, crotchety old fellows who might be stupid enough to take offence at it."

"Allow me, my dear young gentleman, to assure you that the great majority of mankind are those same fidgety, crotchety fellows. No banker would give us the information, and you will excuse us for saying that we could never put ourselves in the way of applying for it."

"Very well, Mr. Tobermory," said Julius, rising. "Now I have got my answer, for my part I do not care a fig about the note, and I give you my word of honor there is not a customer in your bank who is not at perfect liberty to send me a £500 note to-morrow morning, and I pledge myself never to make a single inquiry about the matter. It is my brother's crotchet, this, you know. He has got into a little fix at Forestville, very unjustly I must say, but it has so put him out, poor fellow, that he cannot now even receive a windfall of £500 without making a fuss about it."

"Ha, ha! It is a very hard case indeed," said the banker, laughing.

And Julius, taking his hat, departed with the message to his brother.

As soon as he detailed this conversation to Montagu, the latter opened his eyes. "It is," said he, "very extraordinary that such a thing as this should happen to any man, and still more extraordinary that he should not be able to trace it. However, on this point I am resolved; I will never change that £500 note until I find out from whom it comes."

"Oh! my dear fellow," said Julius, "pray do not trouble yourself by any such scruples as that. Just hand it over to me; I will change it fast enough, and in ten days I will pledge you my honor there shall not be a farthing left of the change."

"Thank you, master Scapegrace," said Montagu, "I am very much obliged to you for your kind offer, but as I know you have got plenty of notes of your own, you will excuse me for not indulging you with any of mine; and now that I have got this reply from London, I will just seal up that note—buy a little cash box for it with a Bramah lock—and deposit it in the bank here. Some day or other I am certain I shall be able to get a clue to it, and until that day comes, master note shall be intact. While I think of it, I will go and put it in safety: I hate to have a sum of money like that in my possession, it might be a temptation for anyone to commit a robbery, and then my hopes of tracing it would be lost."

In pursuance of this resolution, Montagu and his brother went out into the town, bought a cash box, brought it home, and having deposited the £500 note in it, took it off to the bankers, there to await the revelation of this mystery, if it could by any means be obtained.

Day after day, Doem's invitations continued to come upon our hero. Whenever he could escape them, he contrived to do so, but the fact must be admitted that Montagu, like most young men, found the most difficult word in the language to be composed of those two simple letters, N-O, and often when he was quite resolved to keep away from Doem's house, the appearance of the venerable father overcame all resistance, and at six p.m., he once more found his feet under the hospitable mahogany of the aforesaid, in such case made and provided, proctor.

CHAPTER II.

ONE morning, a knock came at Montagu's quarters. "Walk in," said our hero.

The door opened, and in stepped Captain Spinney.

"Ah! Captain Spinney, I am so glad to see you," said Ernest.

"Glad to see me; what are you glad to see me about? You know I do not promise compliments. Man should be sincere in all his dealings, and if sincere, the chances are ten to one he will not get far beyond plain cordiality. Why are you glad to see me?"

"In the first place, Captain Spinney, because you always amuse me. You have the art of saying a great deal without uttering much. In the next place, I see by your face you have something particularly important to communicate this day."

"Psha! was ever man so deceived in his life. Beyond a little matter of gossip, I have nothing to say at all."

"Ah! but what is the matter of gossip?"

"That the decision has come down in your court-martial."

"Nonsense! you do not say so!" said Montagu, seizing Spinney's hand, quite excited. "Is it against me?"

"Perhaps."

"Is there any chance of its being for me?"

"Perhaps."

"Why, it cannot be both."

"Perhaps."

"Why?"

"I suppose I mean what the decision means—everything."

"Who is your informant?"

"Colonel Loosefysh."

"What did he say to you?"

"Nothing."

"O! Spinney, you are Spinney all the world over. Excuse me for taking the liberty of saying so. Now what am I to gather from what you say?"

"This, that, and the other."

"Well, I give you up; you must bring it out in your own fashion. Will you take a cigar?"

"Not if I know it."

"You have had your breakfast, of course."

"Two hours since."

"Where did you see Loosefysh?'!

"In his own quarters."

"What took you there?"

"My legs."

"What did you hear?"

"Much profane swearing."

"Well, sit down, and do not say anything more.

"I shall not sit down, and I shall say something more. I heard from a little bird, yesterday, in town, that the Queen had given her decision on the finding of the court-martial, and that it would reach the regiment to day."

"Well, I am dying to know, but I will not ask a word."

"That is a wise young man; you will know soon enough. However, I made some excuse for calling on Loosefysh this morning, just after I knew he had received the letters by the post, and I could see by the way he was firing and swearing at everything that things had not gone quite as he wished."

"What then, am I acquitted?"

"No, I should say nothing of the sort."

"Well then, what do you say?"

"Nothing."

"Then what has brought you here?"

"To tell you everything."

"Well then, do tell me everything."

"No I shall not."

"Why not?"

"Because I have changed my mind."

"Ah! how cruel of you, Captain Spinney."

"Not at all. The court-martial is summoned to hear her Majesty's decision to-day at twelve o'clock. You will find the decision is not quite so much against you as others hoped, and is not quite so much in your favor as you would have wished. Let that suffice you. Still I can congratulate you on what there is; and when you do go into Court, keep your pluck up, and do not let anyone see that you fear anything; do you understand? That is the only ground on which they can have any pull out of you. Do not you let them see you care a brass button for the whole of them, and once more I congratulate you; but remember, in any future court-martial, not a word about Sweetbreath. Was not that a magnificent fire? Such a splendid shot! Such a shot! Well, you will come to mess this evening, I can tell you. I will keep a chair next me for you. There, good bye; do not say that I have given you any hint of what is coming." And before Montagu could say a single word, down stairs walked Captain Spinney.

Scarcely had he gone, when the door burst vociferously open, and for the first time since the day of the court-martial, in rushed Walduck.

"My dear Montagu, I congratulate you.—The sentence of the finding of the court-martial has come down, and I am quite sure you are acquitted."

"Oh! do you think so, Mr. Walduck?" said Montagu, scarcely turning round. "What makes you think I am acquitted?"

"Because I saw Loosefysh at the window of his quarters just now, looking as black as thunder. I always know when he has some particularly annoying piece of bad tobacco in his pipe, his face tells such tales immediately. If you had been convicted, he would have been cracking jokes loud enough to be heard outside of the barrack square."

"Well," said Montagu, "I do not much care whichever way it is. I think military life is rather a slow sort of affair, and if I am acquitted, not that I expect it, but if I am acquitted, the chances are that I shall sell out immediately."

"Zounds! man, why did not you sell out before this court-martial, and you would have escaped all this bother."

"The reason why I did not sell out, Mr. Walduck, is simply because I was asked to do so, and when people ask things they have no right to ask, I always make a point of refusing them."

"Well, that is accommodating of you, but here is some fellow coming up the stairs."

"Ah! Walduck, my boy, are you here? Montagu, I congratulate you. They say in the regiment that your acquittal has come down."

"Well, I suppose, Captain Worsted, some good news is coming, or I never should have had the pleasure of receiving two visitors in ten minutes, who have never honored my quarters for the last fortnight or so."

"Ah, my dear fellow, etiquette, etiquette, you know. You forget with a man under a sentence of court-martial one must observe a little etiquette."

"Oh, indeed! Ah! etiquette is a charming thing, particularly when it enables you to shew the cold shoulder to an acquaintance."

"Precisely, the cold shoulder—cold shoulder of lamb—cold shoulder of mutton—hard to swallow; you mean to pay us off. Well, give us a cigar; never mind the cold shoulder, that will stand over until next time."

"You will find one in the box at the other end of the room," said Montagu, and Worsted walking over to the box, brought it to the table, and he and Walduck helped themselves.

"Now, Montagu, my boy, open a bottle of

something decent to drink your success and peaceable hearing of your fate."

"Ah! exactly," said Worsted; "as I was coming in here I met Major Fussey, and he assured me it is not an acquittal that has come down. He shook his head very mysteriously, and said it reminded him of the case in which the finding of the court-martial had been reviewed by the Prince of Wales, and, of course, the Prince of Wales was wrapped up in his father."

"Well, never mind the Prince of Wales now."

"Holloa! here comes an orderly."

"Ah, there is a note from the adjutant informing me that the court-martial assembles at twelve o'clock, and that I must be ready to hear the finding of the sentence. With your leave, therefore, gentlemen, while you are smoking your cigars, I will just go into my room and put on my regimentals."

By the time that Montagu's red coat was

donned and he came back to the sitting-room, he found that his two summer-weather friends had flown, having previously finished the bottle, and made a considerable hole in the amount of the cigars.

By a quarter before twelve he issued from his quarters, and there he found his old friend the sentry with the drawn bayonet, who followed him at a respectful distance to the mess room, where the court-martial was already assembled.

The usual formalities having been gone through, the President opened a large letter from the Horse Guards, and, with rather a downcast countenance, read the following missive:

"I am ordered by the Commander-in-Chief to inform you that the minutes, evidence, and finding of the court-martial held on the —— day of —— upon Ensign Montagu, for the charges therein stated, have been laid before her Majesty, who has been pleased to refer the same to her Judge Advocate General. The sentence of the court-martial that the prisoner is not guilty upon the first charge, and that he is guilty upon the second charge, and that he be dismissed her Majesty's service, appearing to be based upon evidence improperly admitted, and the defence of the prisoner impeded by the improper rejection of evidence, it is her Majesty's pleasure that the said finding of the court-martial be annulled. I have the honor to remain, &c., &c., &c.

On hearing this letter read, the worthy members of the court-martial (some looking exceedingly sheepish, and some looking exceedingly wrathful), all rose, and the President putting his hand down by his side, said:

"Under these circumstances, Ensign Montagu, I restore to you your sword."

Ensign Montagu then advanced and received his sword by the hands of the President, and having made a deep bow, slipped the same down into the hole in his sword belt, and with a second stiff bow turned round and left the mess room, never honouring a solitary soul of them with one single word.

CHAPTER III.

Now, thought our hero, as he walked to his quarters, comes the momentous decision. Is not this the right moment to wash my hands of such a service as this, and to address myself to any other occupation in life—to resign and sell out?

While full of these thoughts, and just at the door of his quarters, up came Captain Spinney to him.

"You have heard the good news!"

"Good news. What news?"

"We are ordered out to the Crimea."

"Nonsense," said Montagu.

"Ah! it is no nonsense, my boy. Now is the time when every man may look out for promotion or six feet of sod."

"Ah, well," thought Montagu, "there goes at once all notion of selling out, for to sell out of a regiment going on active service is of course impossible. Nothing now remains but to take the first opportunity of going up to town and finding out who sent me that £500 note, and then I will order everything necessary for our expedition, and take the chances of war for the next few years of my life."

Sitting down and writing a letter to his brother, who had returned to his ship, to tell him the good news, Ernest next applied for a few days' leave, and having obtained it, took the little tin box out of his banker's hands and carried it off to London.

This time he thought he would go to his

friend Tweezer, and learn if he could devise any mode of tracing the note.

"Ah!" said Tweezer, "now this is something like a straightforward business. Here is some ingenuity to be exercised. I would much rather trace this note than defend you before such a rotten tribunal as a court-martial. Now what would be the best way to do it?"

"That is precisely what I leave to you, Mr. Tweezer."

"Well, you are not going back to your regiment to-day; at what hotel are you staying?"

"At Hatchett's."

"I will make some inquiries to-day what is to be done, and write to you there."

From Tweezer's Montagu proceeded to his tailor and accoutrement maker, and in the pleasing occupation of giving orders soon laid the nucleus of a very respectable set of bills.

Next day he received the following note from Tweezer:

"DEAR SIR,

"I have made several enquiries as to the best mode of tracing your £500 note. I have at last devised a mode of doing it. It is rather singular, but if you still insist upon it I suppose it must be done.

"Come to me to-day at eleven o'clock.

"&c., &c."

Punctual to his hour our hero entered Tweezer's office in Lincoln's Inn Fields.

"Now, Mr. Montagu," said the solicitor, "do not be surprised at what I am going to say to you. There is only one mode I find of tracing this note; are you resolved it shall be done?"

"Yes, I am."

"But is it to be done at any cost?"

"Any cost! Zounds, where can be the cost of tracing a bank note?"

"It would be at a very considerable cost, for you must know that the only mode by which we shall be able to overcome the scruples of bankers to disclose their clients affairs is to have the note forged."

"What?" exclaimed Montagu.

"Don't be alarmed; don't be frightened; nobody is going to use the bank note."

"No, I should think not, but you do not seriously propose to me, Mr. Tweezer, to give my consent to have a Bank of England note forged?"

"Whether you give your consent or not is a matter to which I am perfectly indifferent," said Tweezer; "all I can say is, if you do not have it forged, you will never know who it comes from, and if you do have it forged, you can know who it comes from."

"So far as the thing is before me at present," said Montagu, "I utterly spurn it. I shall be no party, in any shape or form, to doing that which is any offence against the laws."

"Ah!" said Tweezer, "the laws are very nice. Now here rises a nice distinction. If a man forges a note with intent to defraud another, that is an offence against the laws; but if a man forges a note merely with a view of testing some scientific experiment, there is no offence against the laws. Now, that is a nice distinction, is it not?"

"That is rather too nice a distinction for me, I confess; and, much as I long to know who sent it to me, I think I shall check my curiosity. But how can it be an offence and no offence?"

"Why, simply in this way, the offence is created by the intention. If I take your hat off your head, merely intending to relieve you of the weight of it, I do you a kindness; but if I take the hat off your head, with the intention of going to sell it, and to put the money in my pocket, it is a felony, it is a theft. Now, you see, if I send this note to a first-rate engraver, and tell him to produce a counterpart of it—it is a very expensive process, I have no doubt, and when I go to the Bank of England, and show them that note, and ask them to be kind enough to tell me whether it is forged or not, they will infallibly say the note is certainly a forged note. They will take possession of the forgery, and I shall then ask them to find out from whom it came. You know, remember, I shall distinctly guard myself, by saying I do not wish the note changed, but to ascertain simply if it is a forged note. I shall give them no information about it, but merely leave them to trace it."

"Well, but, Mr. Tweezer, surely that would be a most ungrateful return to make to the party who sent the note, to set a rumour about that the note was forged, and all the while, we ourselves are forging it."

"But you know there is that little difficulty about the case—it is a difficult case. I do not say, morally speaking, we are right, and I do not see very clearly that there is anything very wrong in the process. Nobody is intended to be hurt by it, and surely it may be supposed to be a very great cruelty to inflict npon the mind of any man, to send him a £500 note anonymously."

"Ah! Ah! Mr. Tweezer, you have got your argument to a nice pitch. I suspect there are not many men in the kingdom who would consider it a very great harm done."

"Ah! but to a sensitive mind like yours what a stimulus to curiosity which you are now suffering. I am sure, sir, you would rather be without this £500 note, for it is of no use to you if you do not intend to spend it."

"I certainly do not intend to spend it, but on the other hand allow me to say I am not at all so clear I would rather not have had it sent me. At any rate, it is rather agreeable and consolatory to think that there is some one takes that amount of interest about one's existence."

"Ah! truly, truly—as far as the feelings

go, possibly so—possibly so—but then you know we lawyers take the feelings very little into account. We go upon everything as a mere business transaction. I do not care, you know, whether you have the note forged, or whether you do not have it forged."

"Precisely, and you would not care whether your client were hanged for forging it or whether he were not hanged."

"Excuse me, sir, there is no hanging in the matter. It is a sort of what shall I call it—a sort of moral morbidity, as to whether a man ought or ought not to raise the veil thrown over this little obscurity. If you wish to know who is the donor, I will get the note forged for you and put it under the nose of the authorities of the Bank of England, and they will sift the truth out, and then, fancy the fun when they think they have got the delinquent—we say, thank you, gentlemen, I merely asked you for information, that is all."

"Yes, but I think the authorities at the

Bank of England are not to be played with in that way. I do not like to have anything to do with affairs of this sort. One never knows, when you deal with such dangerous matters, what motives may be attributed to you by those who hear only half the story. Therefore my decision is, much as I wish to know the party who sent the note, I will have nothing to do with the dangerous plan you have sketched out for tracing it."

"Very well. I think perhaps you are very wise. There is only one other mode in which you might, after a long lapse of time, obtain information about it."

"What is that?"

"I will lay myself out, and see if I can find some party connected with the Bank of England, from whom I might get the information under the rose, and that party might fish it out from the private bank. But you know these things require money—money."

"In other words, you propose to corrupt

all these parties, and give a bribe to one and a bribe to another."

"No; not corruption. Who is corrupt? The Prime Minister gives away an office to an intimate friend's son, who, if not wholly incompetent to the office, is certainly not so competent as many who could be found."

"I suppose that is corruption to some extent."

"The fact is, Mr. Montagu, the world is not so nice as you young gentlemen from school imagine, and if you wish to battle with it, I am sorry to say you must take it as it turns up."

"Then all I can say, Mr. Tweezer, is that the world is a disgusting cheese, full of maggots: and the more I see of it the more I am disgusted with it. So good morning, Mr. Tweezer, good morning."

"Ah! good morning, Mr. Montagu; it is very charming to a hackneyed man of the world like myself, to see a fine, fresh, and generous spirit like yours starting with the first blush of early dawn, and an unsullied sword in your hand, to fight your way through endless victories to high fame and position—it is a charming thing to see. Excuse me detaining your hand in mine for a moment. It is a charming thing quite consolatory to see. But just allow me to say, that between you and that immense distance there lies a tremendous bog, and if you ever attain the object of your ambition it will only be by passing up to your knees in dirt."

"Now then, Mr. Tweezer, as you have been kind enough to pour out upon me your felicitous expressions, just allow me to give utterance to mine."

"Certainly, sir, certainly."

"It is a most disgusting thing for a young man just starting in life to see even in a polished gentleman like you the miserable effects of the hackneying system of mankind. To see men of intellect, men of position, men of independent means, giving themselves up to a course of life where all principles are more or less confounded—nothing is pursued that is straightforward, and the only object thought of is expediency and success. Every man has it in his power in some degree, however slightly, to stand out against this line of conduct, and, though it does not lead to personal gratification at the moment, it must finally lead to self respect and a contented mind, blessings quite as great as any that gratified ambition, or sated wealth can offer. Surely this little sacrifice every man is bound to make, and if every man made it, what a different world it would be from that disgusting specimen we have lately seen before a certain court-martial. Once more, I wish you good morning, Mr. Tweezer."

"Good morning, Mr. Montagu, good morning, and if you ever should grow tired of the army, I know a capital Independent Chapel to be had for that trifle of a £500 note, and from your little specimen of a sermon just now delivered, I have no doubt you would fill the pews to overflowing."

"You be hanged," said our hero, throwing Tweezer's hand away from him with a laugh and running down stairs.

"Mr. Montagu, Mr. Montagu," said Tweezer, runing out of his room, "there is one thing I quite forgot—a matter of business—no joke indeed. Before you go just let me copy perfectly that bank note. Lawyers are always meeting curious odd chances, and if a clue to the mystery should turn up, remember, I will use it."

"Ah! but remember I would not on any account—"

"Oh! yes, I understand all that sort of thing. You may rely upon it that I will do nothing to distress the fair donor, whoever she may be."

"Very well then, under these circumstances, you may keep this copy," and producing the debated security, Mr. Tweezer copied it out in a memorandum book, and the attorney and client parted.

CHAPTER IV.

When Montagu returned to his quarters, he found a note from Mr. Doem, lying upon his table. He opened it and read it. There was something about it which gave him a feeling of surprise, What could be the meaning of it?

"Dear Sir,

"During your absence in town, I called on you once or twice, as I wished to speak to you on a little matter of business. Perhaps you will do me the favor to let me know when you return to quarters, in order that I may make an appointment to meet you."

"What the deuce does this mean?" muttered Montagu; "this does not at all tally with former warm productions, which never contained less than an invitation to dinner, and sometimes to two; however, if it is anything horrible, let us have it out," and he sent a note in reply, to say he should be at home on the following day at eleven o'clock in the forenoon.

Punctual to the moment, a rap came at the door, and in walked Mr. Doem.

After the usual preliminaries of a pinch of snuff and so on, "Mr. Montagu," said Doem, "I have done myself the pleasure of calling upon you, because I understand that the gallant Nonsuch Regiment is ordered to the Seat of War."

"Very true, sir," said our hero, "but I am at a loss to conceive how that can affect you —What is the matter?"

"Well, sir, unfortunately in the destinies of almost every one of our noble regiments the feelings of many members of the community are involved, I may say deeply involved, and in the present instance I am sure you must be prepared for what I have to say, and it is almost unnecessary for me to remind you that you are going to a scene of considerable danger and much peril—personal peril, sir.—I hope you will live to be a personal honor to your country, but during the period that you have been quartered here in the regiment, everyone has observed the degree of marked attention which you have paid my daughter. Now, of course it is not for me to say what your feelings may be; the young ladies, you know, they do not show much; they feel deeply, and I have observed with very great sorrow, that my daughter's happiness and peace of mind are very greatly perturbed at the intelligence of the departure of the gallant Nonsuch, and, therefore, to come at once to the point, I am sure you will meet me with the same frank and gallant spirit with which I come to you. I should really like to know what are your intentions with regard to my daughter ?"

"Really, Mr. Doem, you take me quite by surprise. I have no intentions, except to wish the young lady every health, happiness, prosperity, and all imaginable felicity, not merely during the time the regiment is here, but all the time it remains away, and if ever we should meet again, I should be very happy to show, by every means in my power, how warmly I appreciate your hospitality and kind regards."

"But, my dear sir," said Doem, drawing himself up and looking sternly, "this will not do."

"Won't it?" said our hero.

"Certainly not," said Doem, "I could not think of allowing the affair to end here."

"Why," said Montagu, aghast, "you do

not propose to me another trial, do you? Am I to be treated like an unfortunate pancake—to be loosed out of the frying pan into the fire?"

"Sir, your own conscience may well tell you that an injured father, like myself, cannot submit to have his daughter's affection trifled with. There is such a thing in this country as a jury, which is a very different thing to a court-martial."

"Oh yes, sir," said Montagu, "the devil is represented to wear two horns on his forehead, and I cannot say which is the worst of the two. I have hitherto only sat upon one. Law martial is bad enough, what law civil may be I do not know—it may be a few degrees worse."

"Allow me to say, Mr. Montagu, that this trifling is at least ill-timed. I am sure, sir, whatever you may think, or please to say of the law, this much you must admit, that any humble services of mine were freely offered to you in your late troubles, and I should never have dreamed of looking for costs."

"Oh, of course not," said Montagu. "Indeed, I am quite surprised to hear you mention them. Nobody is aware, I think, that there is such a thing connected with the law as costs. But to revert to the object of your visit, allow me to ask you, Mr. Doem, has your daughter told you that I ever trifled with her affections?"

"I beg to decline to answer any questions, sir, that may commit any party in this matter."

"But, Mr. Doem, if I have trifled with the young lady in her affections, perhaps you will tell me how the thing is done; how do you go to work with a young lady's affections—what does it mean?"

"Why, sir, it means this: when a gentleman of prepossessing exterior and a fascinating address—"

"Oh! really, Mr. Doem, come, you make me blush too deeply."

"No, sir, I merely state the case, not so powerfully as it will hereafter be stated to a jury, but I merely state the case between friends, in the hope that I may avert any unpleasant proceedings."

"Oh! of course."

"Well then, sir, I say that when a gentleman—such a gentleman—following the gallant profession of arms, and admitted into such a distinguished regiment as the gallant Nonsuch, appears before a lady, not only in the full force of these attractions, but backed by those sources of admiration and appearance which the military uniform always confers in the eyes of the female—"

"Oh! in pity spare us; do not talk of 'the female,' Mr. Doem; it spoils all notions of love."

"Well, sir, I will use any other term. In the eyes of ladies generally, I say, sir, that when such a young gentleman is admitted into a family of unmarried ladies, the head of such family may well feel honoured by such an acquaintance, and I see no harm or impropriety in permitting the acquaintance, especially where a gentleman is known to possess such an amount of private property as may render him fit and eligible for the choice of any lady in the land."

"Oh! oh! Mr. Doem, you have got to the property, have you?"

"Of course. You do not think, sir, that I, or any other sensible man, would allow a mere beggarly wearer of a red coat to be perpetually dangling after my daughter, engaging her affections, if when I knew the happiness of the poor girl was irretrievably wrapped up in an honourable settlement in life, the young military gentleman had nothing to support an establishment, and must either be supported out of my purse, or else after a year or two floundering about from barrack to barrack send back my daughter to sit on my knee with half a dozen children."

"Half a dozen children, Mr. Doem," said

Mr. Montagu! "Come, come, now that is rather strong. You count too much upon military prowess. Consider: half a dozen children in two or three years would be twins every year."

"Well, well, sir, you—you—you know what I mean, sir. I do not bind myself to a word or two, but at any rate I am a man of the world, sir. I am a man who has fought my way, sir, I am a man of some little property myself," putting his hand outside his pocket. "Of course I should not have allowed the entrée of my house to be at the disposal of any man that I thought an improper match for my child, and therefore, I say that a gentleman of your position, who is constantly at a man's house—"

"My dear Mr. Doem, it has been at your own invitation."

"Granted that it may have been so; I am bound to show hospitality to the officers of Her Majesty's regiments who come here."

"Yes, but, Mr. Doem, they are not all bound to marry your daughter."

"I do not say they are, sir, I do not say they are, sir. But in this case everybody has been much mistaken if you did not show as much alacrity in winning the young lady's smiles as I could show in inviting you to the house."

"To cut the matter short, do you mean to say that Miss Doem's affections are centered upon myself?"

"You cannot expect any father, sir, to make any admission that is detrimental to the interest of his child."

"Well, well, but let us come to some practical conclusion in this matter. Either the young lady is attached to me or she is not."

"Well, sir, that is a self-evident proposition; that is one step gained."

"Now if the lady is not attached to me, it would be of course most cruel to suppose that there is the least obligation on me to tender an offer of my hand in a quarter where it must necessarily be refused."

"That does not follow, sir."

"But then something follows which is still worse. It would be still more cruel to insist that I should offer my hand to the acceptance of a lady who would accept it without being attached to its possessor—that you cannot expect."

"Well, sir."

"Then you see, if the lady is not attached to me, the object of your visit here is quite premature and out of place. Now, on the other hand, if the lady is attached to me, and your visit is made in consequence of that attachment, why not have the candour to avow it; I should then know what to do."

"What would you do, sir?"

"Excuse me, Mr. Doem. It would be premature to say what I should do until the fact is avowed. Do you mean to say that Miss Doem is attached to me?"

"It does not become me, sir, to speak of the state of any young lady's mind."

"Very sensibly said, Mr. Doem, and that brings me to one mode of terminating this affair. You had better go home to the young lady—tell her that you have seen me about it, and that before I give any answer in the matter whatever, I wish to know that fact—whether the young lady makes any allegation of being attached to me at all. All that I can say is, that I have been very guarded in every thing that has passed between us, and, I assure you, as a gentleman of honor, I have never said one single word to induce the young lady to think I have formed an attachment to her whatever; and I am very much mistaken if she will not do me the justice to say that at any moment; therefore, before I give you my answer to the present application, I have to request that I may see the young lady alone, and that after that she will make to you any communication she thinks fit, and after that, if you choose to prefer your present claims to me, I will give you a decided answer."

"Very well, sir—very well, sir," said Doem. So the matter shall stand. You had better come and dine with us to-day, at six o'clock."

"Oh no, one cannot have peace and war at the same time. Let us first of all finish out this little affair one way or the other, and then if it leaves us on any terms of private intimacy we can then begin the dinner system as soon as you like."

"As you please—as you please—good morning," taking up his hat—then turning back and stepping into the room—"If you will call at my house to-morrow morning at eleven o'clock, my daughter will see you alone."

"I will be there punctual to the moment, Mr. Doem."

Bows were interchanged between both the parties, and the heavy feet of the proctor creaked down the gallant Ensign's stairs.

CHAPTER V.

PUNCTUALLY at eleven o'clock on the following morning, the knocker of Mr. Doem's door sounded with a good round vigorous rat-tat-tat.

"Come," muttered our hero, "there is no trepidation in that at any rate. Now for a pretty scene. Is Miss Doem at home?"

"Yes, sir."

"Will you give my name," said our hero, and he was shewn into the drawing room.

There he found Miss Doem alone, her eyes

were red, and certainly it was only charitable to suppose with weeping. She rose slightly on Montagu's entrance, and then immediately had recourse to a bottle of smelling salts.

"Odds bobs," thought Montagu, "I suppose this will be a case of hysterics presently. What is good for hysterics? Burnt feathers. Now if I had been a staff officer I should have had a fine feather in my hat and I could have burnt it advantageously in the case. As it is I must take my chance."

Miss Doem pointed to a chair, so great was her emotion she was unable to go through her ordinary routine of asking him to be seated.

"My dear Miss Doem," commenced Montagu, "I was very much surprised yesterday by a visit from your Papa, who wanted to know what were my intentions towards you. May I ask if your father came to call upon me by your request?"

The fair Harriet bowed.

"Since you lead me to believe that your father's visit was with your approbation, let me put a further question to you. Have I ever said anything that has led you to imagine I was either attached to you, or seeking to render you attached to me?"

The lady remained mute, and looked very much distressed—had again and again recourse to the smelling bottle, and seemed quite unwilling to make any answer.

"My dear Miss Doem," said Ernest, who perceived that all the lady's gaiety of manner was most mysteriously banished, "if we are to understand each other in this affair, it is quite necessary that you should be able to speak to me; but if you are too unwell to enter upon this discussion now, I will go away; only name a time, and I will call again."

"Pray proceed, I shall be better presently.—The pain of this interview I cannot support a second time," said the fair Harriet, in a die-away tone.

"Am I to understand, then, Miss Doem, that you really expected that I should make any declaration of attachment to you?"

Still the lady was silent.

"I am sorry I am not able to elicit from you any answers to my questions; perhaps it is from the want of ability with which they are put to you, and, therefore, in order to terminate a scene, which, I have no doubt, is very painful to you, and certainly very disagreeable to myself, allow me to say, that whatever feelings I may have once entertained towards you, they were for ever terminated, when I accidentally discovered that the gallant Colonel Loosefysh——" Montagu paused as he uttered these words, and the colour mounted into Miss Doem's cheeks, and gradually overspread her forehead—almost her very eyes seemed blushing, as she drooped them to the ground. "I say when I accidentally discovered that Colonel Loosefysh claimed so large a share of your heart and affections, that you could honour him with a visit at his quarters *tête-à-tête*."

"How dare you, sir, insinuate?" said Harriet Doem, starting at once to her feet, her eyes flashing with fury, and her acting and pretence of a previous fainting manner thrown to the winds—"though I have no brother, sir, to avenge this insult—my father," and she extended her hands towards the bell.

"Stay, Miss Doem, only for a few seconds —I think we can settle this matter without your father—I picked up a glove of yours."

The moment the glove was mentioned, the colour deserted the features of the fair Harriet as rapidly as it had before arisen—even her lips grew pallid; she sank down in her chair and looking at our hero with a horrified glance, waited to hear what further he might say.

"It is unnecessary for me, Miss Doem, to add more. On your return from that evening visit, you dropped a glove. I picked it up, your initials were written in it. I obtained the fellow to it on the following morning, and therefore allow me to say—tho' this shall never pass my lips to anyone unless you compel me to declare it—allow me to say that I think if you have a claim upon the declarations of attachment of anyone, it is on those of Colonel Loosefysh, and not of myself. I do not seek to put any unkind construction on what I have seen, that is not for me to do; you may be perfectly able to explain it, but I do not wish you to do so for a moment, but I think, under all the circumstances, perhaps our wisest course will be for you to assure your father, without stating to him any reason, that you are perfectly satisfied with the explanation I have given you this morning, and for me to abstain from making to him, or any other person, unless you expressly desire it, any communication on this subject whatever. Should you think otherwise, you will write to me. I thank you for all your past good offices, and I wish you every future prosperity and happiness."

Making a low bow, Montagu quietly walked to the door, leaving the fair Harriet with her head thrown back in the chair in which she sat, gazing in vacancy, and the color alternating on her cheek from deep red to a livid purple.

"Thank heaven, I am out of that scrape," muttered he, as he closed the door behind him.

CHAPTER VI.

But Ernest's thankfulness speedily received a disastrous check, when, popping out of a room close at hand, there loomed upon his sight the monster apparition of fat old Doem himself.

Poor Ernest had thought to get to the front door and make off, attain his quarters, order out his horse, and get a long and solitary ride. Instead of this pleasure, he now beheld the unwieldly bulk of old Doem, opening his study door—his sanctum sanctorum—his den of abomination lined with law books and filled up with musty parchments, lying here and there like the bones of dispatched victims, while Doem himself with a solemn air that was enough to unnerve most men, motioned with his hand into this acherontic cavern and said—

"Will you allow me a few words, Mr. Montagu?"

"It is quite unnecessary, Mr. Doem," said Ernest with an air of assumed hilarity, "if you will just speak to your daughter, Miss Doem, you will find everything arranged to her satisfaction."

"Ah! Oh! Hem—ahem—my daughter's satisfaction, you said, Mr. Montagu. Do I understand you that you are going to be—" and there old Doem paused, looking unutterable things into the eyes of our hero.

"Attention! As you were!" said Ernest. "Yes, precisely, Mr. Doem—Stand at ease!" and he drew a long breath like a man just relieved of the night-mare.

"Really, sir, this jesting is very incomprehensible. Do me the favor to walk into my study for a few minutes while I see my daughter."

"Really, Mr. Doem," said our hero putting up his hands, "I should be quite grieved to occupy your valuable time. You can write to me, you know after you have seen your daughter; it would be quite——"

"Nay, Mr. Montagu, excuse me. Nothing can be more important to you or to me than this matter, and while such an unpleasant affair is *in transitu*, do let us give our attention to it for a few minutes like men of business, in order that we may dispatch it in one way or the other. Now, do me the favor to walk into my room and I will be with you in a few minutes," and fat old Doem contrived to surround Montagu with such an air of insinuation, entreaty and compulsion, that in a few seconds our hero found himself in the den aforesaid, looking on the musty parchments, while old Doem hurried into the next room to his daughter.

"What a fool I was," thought Ernest, "to yield compliance to that fellow's wish, and come in here: I have a good mind to open the door and slip away, but then, let me see, will not that look like a case of guilty knowledge, and very undignified in an officer holding Her Majesty's commission."

While he was yet debating what to do, in came Doem, most excited.

"Really, Mr. Montagu, I do not understand what you have said to my daughter."

"Said to your daughter, Mr. Doem?"

"Yes, sir, to my daughter—What have you said to my daughter?"

"Well, sir, it is very soon explained. I have said to your daughter what most gentlemen say to ladies—good morning, how do you do, and I wish you good bye."

"No, sir, I cannot, I will not be trifled with in this way. What have you said to my daughter which has produced this extraordinary state of mind?"

"Excuse me, Mr. Doem; when I asked to be with the lady alone for a few minutes, it was expressly for the purpose of making a communication to her without also making it to you, and I certainly shall not repeat a single word that has passed between us. Had I intended otherwise, you might have been present at the interview."

"Really, sir, I do not understand this—I do not understand this conduct."

"That is very possible, Mr. Doem, neither do I understand being detained in your house. So if you will be pleased to open the door, I will leave it."

"Pardon me, Mr. Montagu, if I was abrupt for a few seconds—you know what a father's emotions are, sir. This is my daughter, sir, my only daughter, my only child; I have no son, sir, she is my daughter and son in one—I have no wife, sir,—she is my daughter and my son and my wife. She is everything to me, sir, and if anything happens to me, sir, I shall leave that lady a handsome fortune. Conceive then, sir, how distressing it is to me to find that your attentions have been the talk of the whole neighbourhood, and, that my daughter's—— I won't say her name, but her position is compromised, and now you not only tell me that you never meant anything like attention, but, when I go to ask the young lady for an explanation of your interview, all that she can mutter to me is—'something between you and Colonel Loosefysh.' "

"Oh! does she say anything about Colonel Loosefysh?" said Montagu, in the most astonished manner possible.

"What she said, sir, or what she meant, I do not know. She certainly muttered the name of Loosefysh."

"Well you know, Mr. Doem, if she says anything about Colonel Loosefysh, I suppose she means you to go and ask Colonel Loosefysh what his intentions are."

"Ask Colonel Loosefysh his intentions," muttered Doem, looking at our hero as if he would like to eat him up.

"Yes, Mr. Doem, you seem to be perfectly master of the process which is gone through in these little matters, why not ask the Colonel; I daresay he would give you an answer just as well as an Ensign."

"I do not understand you, Mr. Montagu."

"And I do not understand you, Mr. Doem. I never did understand you. I never shall be able to understand you; and, under these circumstances, therefore, you will excuse me, wishing you a good deal of happiness and a little less obscurity," and, by a sudden movement, Ernest got the handle of the door in his hands, opened it, and was in the passage before fat old Doem could intercept him.

No sooner had he got into the passage

than he sprang to the front door and opened its fastening.

"Mr. Montagu, Mr. Montagu," said Doem, coming out into the passage.

But Ernest was too knowing to make any reply; closing the door he hurried down the steps into the little garden that intervened between the road and house.

"Ah! Mr. Montagu," said Miss Wyndham who stood over a rose tree from which she had just severed a blossom and was now engaged in gazing intently on the parent tree.

"How do you do, Miss Wyndham?" said Montagu, who could nct avoid speaking to her before he left the premises, and, then, as we all say the first thing that comes uppermost when we are thinking of something very different, he added; "what are you gazing at so intently, Miss Wyndham?"

"A very interesting spectacle," said that young lady.

"What is that?" said our hero.

"A poor young fly who has just made his escape from the web of an old spider in this rose bush, and no sooner had the fly got away than the old spider popped out of his hiding place and shook the web with rage—very interesting is it not, Mr. Montagu?"

Ernest looked in Miss Wyndham's eyes for a few minutes and read there a strange and laughing intelligence.

"Well," thought our hero, "dear me, I have been a very foolish fellow. I never saw that those eyes were so bright before, and the story of the spider and the fly must mean old Doem and myself."

"To say nothing of the spider, Miss Wyndham, you have a very pretty rose in your hand. Will you bestow it as a parting gift to a poor cavalier who is ordered to the East?"

"What to the seat of war?" said Blanche, her look assuming an earnest expression and her lip quivering for a second in a way that Montagu could not quite comprehend.

"Yes, to the seat of war, Miss Wyndham; so you must give us your warmest congratulations and your best prayers."

"My best prayers certainly—but for my congratulations also, I suspect that few of us, in this country, know the miseries to which you are hastening. Oh! why did you not take my advice weeks ago when an opportunity occurred of leaving such a profession and getting out of it with credit."

"That is just the question, Miss Wyndham, on which we are all at issue. Where can be the credit to a soldier of wearing the uniform in time of peace, and then when the real hour for the hero comes, pulling off the armour that calls him to a post of danger."

"Well I am truly sorry for this intelligence, I would say—take care of yourself, but, alas! that in your position is impossible."

"And I say to you, Miss Wyndham, do not forget your observation on the rose tree, though one fly has got out of the spider's net, I fear that one is left behind."

"Alas!" said Blanche, with a sigh. "I fear so too, for while it is the lot of some flies to escape these toils, it is the doom of many others to perish in them."

As these words were uttered, Blanche and her companion reached the gate.

There was a tone of feeling in her voice and expression in her countenance which made a strange feeling in the heart of Montagu, and his hand lingered over hers as he wished her good bye. The rose bud still lingered in her fingers, and, gently detaching it, he fastened it in the button hole of his breast. As he did so, was it chance, or was it something nearer to fact that painted in Montagu's eye, a tear on Blanche Wyndham's cheek, but whichever it may have been, it was only the glitter of a moment.

In another instant she had turned away her head and hurried back to the house.

"What a fool I have been," thought Ernest, as he went back to his quarters. "I do believe, after all, that there is the pearl of the oyster which I have utterly overlooked, while amusing myself with gazing on the fleeting, fictitious light of the shell."

Determined to work out these musings he proceeded to his stables, threw himself upon his horse's back, and was soon immersed in the shadow of the neighbouring forest.

CHAPTER VII.

The progress of our story induces us, like all other brother novelists, to do the strictest justice to our *dramatis personæ*. Hitherto we have lavished all our care and attention upon the illustrious Plantagenet, giving him the full precedence of the military services, and, it is now fully high time that we should bestow some little regard upon what was done by the younger brother, Julius Scapegrace, of Her Majesty's ship Saucebox.

The Saucebox had been commissioned by the first lieutenant at Portsmouth. She took some little time to fit out, and owing to a little affair of parliamentary influence at the Admiralty, some time elapsed before her captain was appointed.

At last, however, that night the question was decided. Mr. Barter, who represented the important constituency of Brawlbrook, had at last given a desirable vote at an hour of need. It was thought wonderful by some people how he should have contrived to put the Ministry under so marked an obligation to him, but those were blunderers that mused over the matter. The member for Brawlbrook was a Scotchman. How could he fail, when he gave his vote, to give it at the very nick of time when he could be sure to acquire the utmost possible amount of consideration for that which he bestowed.

This vote was given on Tuesday night and on Wednesday morning his cousin, Captain McCrotchet, of course a brother Scot, received a letter at his club requiring him to repair instantly to Portsmouth and hoist his pennant on board the Saucebox.

The news travelled quickly down to Portsmouth and was communicated by the first lieutenant at the dinner table of the wardroom mess.

"I say, my boys," said the first lieutenant, "our skipper is appointed, and I never heard his name before, but I suppose he is in the Navy List. Captain McCrotchet. Did you ever hear of him, Simpson?" appealing to the old captain of marines.

"I? never—egad it is rather an ominous name too."

"Did you ever hear of a Captain McCrotchet, Wetherell?" applying to the second lieutenant.

"No, I never heard such a name."

"Strange, a man should be appointed to a ship, that nobody has ever heard of before. I always understood that Captain Smith was going to hoist his pennant over us."

"Ah! no, I began to doubt it yesterday when I saw the Times," said Mr. McMurdo, the surgeon.

"Why what could you see in the Times to make you think he would not be appointed to the ship?"

"Why I saw that his father had voted against Government on the Nunnery Bill."

"Ah! that is the way the Service is now going to Old Harry headlong. A man may be the best officer and seaman that ever broke biscuit, yet, if some infernal relation gives a wrong vote, or does not toady to the minister at the right time, his claims are overlooked in a moment. So I suppose this is the way Captain McCrotchet has got the ship"——but here prudence suggested to the lieutenant to stop short, when he added, "Well I hope this McCrotchet is a smart fellow, though I never heard of him before. McCrotchet — McCrotchet—a curious name, McCrotchet."

"I have heard of it, sir, very often," said

Scapegrace, who was that day a guest, dining in the wardroom.

"You have heard of it, have you, why, where the deuce should you have heard of it?"

"I often used to hear my father mention him—they both belonged to the United Service Club."

"Oh! What did you hear your father say of him? What sort of a fellow did your father say he was?" said the marine officer.

"Oh! he used often to laugh at him very heartily. His account of him was that he had always sixty good reasons for never doing a kindness to anyone."

"Well, that is a blessed disposition to have in a captain's cabin," grumbled the first lieutenant. "How old is he, youngster?"

"I do not know, I never saw him, but I suppose by his being a contemporary of my father's, he must be about fifty."

"Ah! I will look at the Navy List presently. That is the man, is it. What countryman is he?"

"Oh! you need never ask that," said McMurdo, "such a man as this young gentleman describes can only be a fellow countryman of mine; he must be born in Scotland."

"Well, Mac, there is one consolation you will have the physicking of him at any rate; perhaps you will be able some day to physic the sixty reasons out of him."

"When is he going to join the ship?" asked the marine officer.

"I should think he will be down to-morrow morning," said the first lieutenant.

"O, take my word for it," said McMurdo, "you do not comprehend the man at all. Among naturalists—show them only the bone of a creature's tail, and they will draw you the whole skeleton directly; so from the one little anecdote of our young friend there, I prognosticate that Captain McCrotchet will be a-board this ship to-night."

"Zounds! you do not mean that, Mac?"

"I do though, and the only thing he will regret, will be that his cabin is not all ready for him to sleep in, to save him the expenses of an hotel."

At this very moment there was heard a voice shouting from the upper deck, "Sideboys! Sideboys! Sideboys! Down below there!"

"Run on deck, you rascals," was heard from the boatswain's mate.

"Why, what is that?" said the first lieutenant. "What did the boatswain's mate say?"

"I think, sir, he said that the captain is alongside," said Scapegrace.

"Oh! impossible."

"Ah, Ha!" said McMurdo, "did not I tell you so? I know the habits of the animal perfectly well. I could even take a pen and ink and draw it on paper."

"Confound it," said the first lieutenant, starting up.

"Stay, Heathfield,—stay. Let me describe him to you. First of all, he has got sandy whiskers; he is a little, thick-set man, with a very smooth face, shaved sharp, and a kind of piggish countenance."

"Hush, hush, doctor—doctor, this is carrying the joke too far."

"Please, sir, Captain McCrotchet is on the quarter deck," said the mate of the watch, presenting himself.

"Very well, sir, I am coming," answered the first lieutenant, and, going on deck the first lieutenant found precisely the individual that McMurdo had drawn.

A gentleman in a blue coat, black hat, well polished boots, trousers nicely fitting over them, a sort of light brown waistcoat, and one of those smooth, oval, pudding like faces where all the muscles are nicely fitted out to an unenviable uniformity; the hair cut short on the forehead, the eyes small, the nose large, and just a little bit of red sandy whiskers fringing the extremity of the jaw.

The moment the first lieutenant appeared on the quarter deck, this individual, who was rather under than above the middle height, drew himself up with a great deal of rigidity, and, in answer to the half bow or inclination of the body of the first lieutenant, he said: "Mr. Heathfield, I presume?"

"That is my name," said the first lieutenant.

"Very good, I am Captain McCrotchet; I have come down from the Admiralty to hoist my pennant on board this ship. I am sorry the short notice I have had has precluded the possibility of sending my furniture down to my cabin. I cannot sleep on board, therefore, to night, but to-morrow morning, at 9 o'clock I shall return, read my commission to the crew, and hoist my pennant accordingly."

"Very well, sir, every thing shall be in readiness. In the mean time we are just sitting down to dinner in the wardroom, will you do us the honor of joining us."

"Weel, Mr. Heathfield, I will just tak a snack with ye, as I have only just come from the train, and I have not ordered any dinner at my hotel. You seem to have the ship in very fair order considering what a short time you have been in commission."

"In a few days, sir, you will be able to report her ready for sea. Will you go first, sir, or shall I shew you the way?"

"I will follow you, Mr. Heathfield."

As soon as Heathfield got down on the lower deck the noise of laughing and joking and the clatter of knives and forks was very distinct in the wardroom.

"You seem to be very merry among yourselves, Mr. Heathfield."

"Well, Captain McCrotchet, I am happy to say, we have hitherto proved a very united mess. We get on very well together, and I think your officers will meet your approval." Then stepping rapidly to the door, for fear that anything should be heard that ought not to be heard, he said in a loud voice, "Captain McCrotchet, gentlemen, does us the honour to join our table to-day."

In an instant, a dead silence fell over the assembly. Even the boys, the officers' servants, ceased to clatter their plates and knives and forks for a brief space, as they turned to look at their commander: the conversation ceased, and every officer arose from his chair.

"Pray be seated, gentlemen, pray be seated," said McCrochet, with that studied endeavour to avoid the Scotch accent, which is often remarkable among emigrants from the northern clime.

"I hope, Captain McCrotchet, you will excuse the rough way in which we must entertain you. Our mess is hardly formed as yet, and we could not have anticipated the pleasure of so soon seeing our Captain. I only heard a few minutes ago that you were appointed."

"Preceesely," said McCrochet, "I only heard myself of the appointment this morning; but, in Her Majesty's service, I have always thought it a good rule to do that which others are thinking about. What is your name, youngster?" said the Captain, seating himself next to Scapegrace.

"My name, sir, is Julius Montagu Scapegrace: I was mate of the afternoon watch to-day, and the first lieutenant was kind enough to invite me to dine with him."

"Verra gude, verra gude, Montagu. Are you any relation to an old General Montagu, that I remember at the United Service Club?"

"Yes, sir, his second son."

"Oh, indeed! Indeed, I am verra glad I have you in my ship. Your father and I often used to have a crack at the club together."

"Yes, sir, I have heard him mention your name. I was just telling the first Lieutenant.

You recollect what I was saying Mr. Heathfield?"

A general smile went round the table at these words, and the first Lieutenant looked especially confused at this act of impudence.

"Oh! you were telling them that you had heard your father mention me. Well now, come, what did your father say of me? What did you tell them?"

"Well, Captain McCrotchet, I said that my father used to say of you—" and here the impudent youngster looked all round the table at the horrified faces of his auditory, who could scarcely believe it possible that any lad would go so far, and wondering whether he would be fool enough to repeat *verbatim* what he had said before.

"Well, sir, what did your father say of me?"

"Well, sir, I do not intend to quote his exact words, but he said you had always sixty good reasons for taking up a well defended position."

At this termination of the speech, the youngster looked round the table again, and all the assembled officers seemed to relieve themselves by breathing freely.

"Ah!" said McCrotchet, "I remember very well. The old General and myself used to have what I call a strategic crack. He was a dashing, daring officer; and that which you say reminds me, that I always used to take up the defensive. He used frequently to compliment me by saying, whenever he commanded an army, I should be General of the Rear Division, with a Corps of Royal Marines."

"I do not remember anything about the Marines, but I have no doubt, sir, he would have put you in the rear," said the impudent youngster.

"What makes you think that, boy?" said Mc Crotchet rather sharply.

"That is, I mean in a retreat, sir, because it is the post of honour."

"Ah! verra gude,—yes, yes. And how is your father?"

Julius did not answer for a moment, and his countenance changed.

"How is the old man?"

"Poor fellow, sir, he died some months ago."

"Oh! he is dead. Ah! dear me. I am very sorry for your loss. He was a fine, gallant, liberal-hearted fellow, and gave some of the best dinner-parties of any man in London. I think I used to see some brothers and sisters of yours, used I not?"

"Yes, sir," said Scapegrace. "I had one brother, who has gone into the army, and my sisters are residing at our house in town with one of their aunts."

"Well, that is very droll, very droll, that you should have been able to give a good character of me to my junior officers from my old friend, the General."

"Very singular indeed, sir," said the youngster, looking hard at the first Lieutenant, who, in order to preserve his gravity, made a direct change of the subject by challenging his guest to a convivial potation.

"Captain McCrochet, will you allow me to have the honor of a glass of wine?"

"Indeed I shall be verra glad of a glass of wine, Mr. Heathfield," said the Captain, filling himself a bumper, and tossing it off with the air of a man who is conscious of having made a very favourable impression on his beholders.

The Captain now challenged the Master to a glass of wine, and put some questions as to the stowage of the hold, the water, and provisions, from which point the conversation took a decidedly professional turn; till, the cloth being cleared, and the wine put on the not-as-yet-very-bright mahogany, the first lieutenant gave the health of Her gracious Majesty, the Queen. This toast being drained with all that heartfelt loyalty which gallant tars feel for a Sovereign, not only excellent in herself but celebrated for her love of the briny ocean, a slight pause ensued which Captain McCrotchet broke. "Gentlemen," said he, "allow me to propose, Success to H. M. S. Saucebox, and may we soon be in all the thickest of the Russian War." This toast was also warmly honored, and opened up such a crop of discussion and stories as required no further stimulus. Many of the officers commented on the unkind conduct of the Americans, in siding so unequivocally with a despotic government against their own parent country.

"They will be paid off in their own coin soon," said young Scapegrace.

"How do you mean?" enquired the Captain.

"Why, sir, simply this—that before many years have passed over their heads, they will all be drawing daggers at one another's throats. The Northerners already hate the Southerners to such an extent, there is no abuse in the vocabulary they do not expend in describing each other to strangers. Law and order are things for which they do not even profess the slightest respect. Slavery and trade are both subjects on which all their feelings and interest are opposed; and the whole United States, when I travelled in them with my father, remined me of a powder-magazine, with a bonfire burning at the door. So long as they can keep the door shut, well and good; but the moment the door opens in will go the sparks, and all be blown to the skies in a jiffey."

"So, youngster, you travelled in the States, did you?"

"Yes, sir; my father spent fourteen months there with me, or I rather with him."

"In that time you must have seen something. Tell us what made the most impression on your mind of all you saw there."

"Well, sir, so many things impressed themselves on my mind in that go-ahead country, and life altogether is, if I may use the term, so exaggerated, compared with our own old world notions, that every thing smacks of a nightmare; but I think a love-adventure, that happened in an hotel where we were then staying, though not at the time we were there, but which was told me by one of the guests—"

"A love adventure! Come, come, that's the very thing for wine and walnuts; and told by a boy of fourteen, our morals ought to be safe."

"Oh sir, I would not hurt your morals for the world!" saucily answered Scapegrace. "The gentleman who told me the story, admitted that he had wrapped up the names of the parties to disguise as much as possible their identity, and had also laid the scene in a different locality from that where it occurred, because, he added with a wink, these Southerners are very free in the use of their bowie-knives, if you repeat any thing they don't fancy. My informant gave the story as follows:

A young and wealthy planter of Virginia

had a large estate that came down to the sea; and just before his father died, and he came into full possession, a neighbouring and much smaller property was bought by a Spanish emigrant, Don Andrea Cattaba, who, having been very unfortunate in gambling on the stocks, had been obliged to give up an appointment in the island of Cuba, and had bought a worn out property called Troumaca, the estate to which I have alluded. The young planter's name was Worsley, he was very tenacious of tracing his descent from a Yorkshire family; and the name of his property, which was certainly a very splendid one, was "Southwolds Bluff." Don Andrea was deceived in his purchase, the house was greatly wanting repair, the estate considerably run out, and the negroes old and neglected. The last owner had been an absentee; the cheap price of the property had tempted the Spaniard, and he soon found that he had only emigrated to Virginia to wage in a more disagreeable form the same battle with poverty that had frightened him away from Cuba.

Unequal to the task of managing his estate alone, he sent to Madrid for his nephew, Don Ottavio Cattaba, under whose superintendence affairs rapidly improved. The real secret of his improvement being this—the old Spaniard had one child, a beautiful girl of sixteen, named Ivola. Up to the time of the nephew's arrival, young Worsley had been somewhat attentive to Ivola, whose mother, in a quiet way, had encouraged his addresses.

The old lady saw very naturally that her husband's health was infirm, that the two estates would amalgamate very advantageously, and that Mr. Worsley would form an unexceptionable son-in-law for her.

Immediately on the nephew's arrival, this comfortable prospect became clouded, some mutual, overwhelming attraction instantly drew Ivola and Ottavio together. The nephew found her counsel and assistance necessary in everything, while she suddenly manifested an interest and an aptitude for the details of a planter's county life, which brought them incessantly together. Their near relationship, and residence under the same roof, gave them endless opportunities of being together; and before three weeks were over, both were irremediably overpowered by the strongest and most delightful of all intoxications, love.

Mr. Worsley and his fine estate were utterly forgotten by the lovers, not so by Mamma or Worsley himself. Up to the time of Ottavio's arrival, he had been giving himself the airs of an eligible *parti*, had spoken of Donna Cattaba's 'wish to catch a rich husband for her daughter,' &c., &c. No sooner, however, did he behold the evident attachment of the handsome Ottavio to his beautiful cousin, than the keenest pangs of jealousy in his own breast told him too plainly how deeply he himself was attached to Ivola, and with what folly he had thrown away his own happiness. Every little attention in his power he now displayed, but they met no response from the enamoured Donzella. He then had recourse to superb presents to the mother, who espoused his suit, but with no success to her daughter. Young Worsley then, with great want of generosity, made a proposal in due form to the father, who at once sent for his child, and requested her to accept this opportunity of so suitably settling herself in life.

Luckily Ottavio had foreseen what was coming, and prepared Ivola how to act on the emergency. Receiving her parents' communication with great respect, she said, with undeniable truth, that the step proposed was the most important in life, that it required grave consideration, that she would think over how far she and Mr. Worsley could contribute to one another's happiness, and begged her father to allow her all the time for deliberation in his power.

The father well knew his wife had a will of her own, which always grew the stronger the more it was opposed; very prudently, therefore, he accorded to Ivola any time for reflection she might require, contenting himself with begging that she would interpose no unnecessary delay. Ivola withdrew from her father's study without another word, ran into the garden where she knew Ottavio was sure to be waiting for her, found him hidden in the foliage of a luxuriant magnolia tree, carving her name, for the hundredth time, on its smooth stem, threw herself into his arms, and burst into tears.

Ottavio was a man pre-eminently of energy and action. He saw what an opportunity was in his power for striking an irrecoverable blow against the enemy, and seized it without shrinking. Worsley was a protestant, the Cattabas staunch papists. For the sake of Worsley's wealth, they were ready to waive their scruples, professing to believe that his wife would convert him. Not so thought the family Confessor, who had more than once been deeply offended by Worsley's ridicule of Catholic ceremonies. On the other hand, Ottavio had secured this priest's friendship, made him his confidant, and obtained his promise to assist him in any difficulty that might arise.

Before Ivola's tears were dry, Ottavio had obtained her consent to an immediate and private marriage, as the only mode af securing her from the persecutions of Worsley.

When the priest was informed of this promise and implored to celebrate the ceremony, he seemed staggered, and took a night to consider the question. Thinking, however, from the awkward position of all the parties, that speedy marriage was the least dangerous result to be apprehended, his reverence, on the following morning, consented to the lovers' prayers, and married them. The great difficulty now was to break this intelligence to the father. Ottavio pondered well the various difficulties to be surmounted; and then, following the dictates of a brave and generous heart, went straight to Worsley, asked his friendship and assistance, and confided to his rival the fact that Ivola was already his bride as well as cousin.

Had Worsley been formed in a mould similar to that of Ottavio, all would have gone well, and much happiness might have been in store for these young neighbours; but unfortunately he was not so. Worsley had been educated by weak and silly parents as their idol—the valued heir who was to succeed to a great property, and whose hopes or wishes none were to cross. As he listened to the narration of Ottavio, a stranger might have detected, in his dark and expressive face, feelings of a frightful malignity and revenge, mingled with traces of cruelty and cunning, that boded ill for the newly-married couple.

To Ottavio's great surprise, he coldly promised to observe the strictest silence as to the confidence reposed in him, yet in the same breath refused all credence to the tale of their marriage. In vain Ottavio offered to take him to the priest. An incredulous smile, a polite bow, and the assurance that he was "too good," was the only response. Ottavio thought over this singular reception of his confidence for a few minutes. It was quite clear Worsley would never be his friend. It was equally clear that nothing could be got by making him an open enemy; and so, with some commonplace expressions of courtesy, they separated.

On the following morning, Worsley called on Ivola's father, to renew his suit, and ask for his answer to the offer he had made, hinting at the same time his fears that his own suit would never prosper while Ottavio remained in the same house, and suggesting that the father and mother should take their daughter on a visit to New York, and leave Ottavio to manage the estate in Virginia.

Don Andrea had always entertained a great dislike to cousins marrying. An engagement between his child and nephew had never occurred to him. The bare mention of an attachment between them put him in a fury, which was little calmed by remembering that Ottavio was only a younger son, in no way a promising match, and wholly dependent on his own exertions for success. He at once accepted the proposal of Worsley to go from home, and to separate the cousins. This he did the more readily, as it afforded him an opportunity of taking the opinion of an eminent physician residing at New York, whom he had long wished to consult on his own health.

When the young couple heard this resolution, they were, of course, very much perplexed. Ottavio was for taking the bold course, and at once declaring their marriage;

but, unfortunately, Ivola shrank from this decided step, and trusted rather in a more timid policy, to gain the sanction of her parents. On one point alone they were agreed, which was to abridge their separation as much as possible, and that Ottavio should speedily follow his wife.

On reaching New York, Don Andrea went to one of the largest hotels, and there took up his abode. The apartment, selected with much care, for Ivola, was one on the third floor, leading from that of her mother; while Mr. Worsley, who joined them the day following their arrival, had rooms on the story above.

Scarcely had Ottavio received intelligence of these facts, than he hurried off to New York. Arriving there in the evening, he disguised himself as well as he could in a large cloak, and made a hasty reconnoissance of the exterior of the hotel. He had previously written to Ivola, to be at her window, watering some flowers, as the clock struck eight.

Punctual to a moment, Ottavio was on the spot, saw his dear little wife at the occupation prescribed for her, saw also that she recognised him; and then entering the hotel, engaged rooms, which, though more distant than he liked, were as nearly as he could get them above her own.

As soon as Ottavio had taken possession of his quarters, he opened the window, and leaning over saw that he was separated by two floors, and a distance of six windows, from his wife's chamber. As it was impossible to communicate with her from the interior of the house, except by going through her mother's room; and as communication with her from the exterior of the hotel was dangerous to madness, his journey from the South to New York seemed almost fruitless.

But Ottavio resolved, that no impediments should deter him. On the story next but one below his, which was the fourth from the ground, or, as it is commonly called, the

"Third floor," there ran a bold projecting cornice of stone—at a height from the ground so dizzy that the heart grew sick while the eye measured it—only a few inches wide, and where few men could have walked even had there been a rail to hold on by. This cornice ran directly past his wife's window, and on it stood the flowers she had that evening tended, and which served most conveniently to mark out her locality. This cornice Ottavio resolved at all hazards to make that night his road.

Going out once more, he provided himself with a quantity of the strongest harpooning line, and getting it stretched and tested as well as the brief space allowed, conveyed it to his room. The line was calculated to bear about four times his own weight. Making fast the end of this very securely to his bedstead, and jamming the latter up with chairs, so that it could not well move, he buckled round his waist a strong leather belt, which he was accustomed to wear. He then proceeded to make numerous knots in the strands of the harpoon line, to insert between them little strips of a worsted stocking, which he cut up for the purpose, very similar to the tufts of wool which are interwoven in the ropes used for belfry purposes.

His preparations being now complete, he waited patiently till midnight, a time when he knew his uncle and aunt were in all probability asleep. Fastening the line to his belt, and taking a coil of it round his left arm, he got as quietly as possible out of his window and began to lower himself towards the cornice.

Up to this time, Ottavio had imagined that no one possessed the secret of his arrival; but he had to deal with an antagonist of the greatest cunning. Not only had Worsley surrounded him by spies at Troumaca, who sent him by post, intelligence of every movement, but he had been actually dogged to the very door of his own room ten minutes after his instalment. Worsley knew the number of his rival's apartment, and read in the absent and confused expression of the bride, perfect confirmation of the news.

Convinced that Ottavio could only have come to the hotel to communicate with his wife without the knowledge of her parents, and having wormed out of her mother the exact position of her bedroom, Worsley at once jumped to the conclusion that Ottavio would that night try to escalade her apartment by the window. Daring as he knew the Spaniard to be, the Southerner scarcely ventured to hope that his rival would risk such a fool-hardy attempt.

In full expectation of seeing him dashed to pieces, Worsley took himself off to his room, as soon as Don Andrea and his party had retired.

By a lucky coincidence for Ottavio, the window of Worsley was not directly below his own, but three windows nearer to the bride's: instead therefore of having to slide down before Worsley's window in order to reach the cornice, he only had to walk below it and before it, after the cornice was safely reached.

In younger days, Ottavio served for two years as midshipman on board a Spanish frigate, and nothing but the education of a seaman could have prompted such a fearful undertaking or given him the least chance of success.

The moon was shining brilliantly in the dark blue sky, and that quarter of the city was rapidly sinking to repose, as Ottavio, with a silent prayer, let fall a few coils of the rope, till it reached the giddy ledge; then, twisting a silk handkerchief round that part of it which rested on the stone window-sill, lest it should be worn or cut by the friction, he slipped down the line, hand under hand, as rapidly as possible, lest he should be observed by any one in the windows he had to pass, and stood in safety on the hideous cornice: but here the real perils of his adventure began.

If he walked in the usual manner, the breadth of his shoulders would overbalance his weight, and hurl him instantly into the space below. He could no longer derive support from the line, for that would pull him in the opposite direction. The stones of the wall were so smoothly jointed, he could find no support from them. If he faced the house and walked on tiptoe, the least trip would throw the balance of his body down into the street: on the other hand, if he turned his back to the wall, the appalling sight of the depth below might act upon his brain and turn him giddy. Nevertheless the last alternative was the one he determined to adopt.

Cautiously turning round with his back to the building, and stilling the tumult of his heart by a strong effort of will, Ottavio stood quite erect, the back of his head just touching the stones; and then advancing his left foot a few inches sideways, he carefully brought his other foot up beside it; and very slowly repeating this operation, he in this way had proceeded past two windows, at a snail-like pace, letting fall, from time to time, sufficient line to allow of his sidling advance.

No sooner, however, had Ottavio's window been slowly opened to commence his descent, than Worsley noiselessly unfastened his casement and set himself to watch, abstaining from shewing more of his head than was necessary just to catch sight of his rival. He soon saw all the difficulties with which the latter had to contend: but the dauntless and clever manner in which they were encountered filled his soul with the utmost dread that the husband would succeed in his enterprise.

Jealousy, intensified to madness, racked his heart deeper and deeper at every fresh step with which Ottavio stole onward to his bride;

and as he had his back turned to the wall, Worsley was able, unobserved, to lean out over, and note at full leisure the agonising spectacle of his supplanter's approaching triumph. As moment after moment crept by, the Southerner, in the wildness of his hatred and despair, kept wishing for Ottavio's fall, and turning over in his own mind how it could be best accomplished.

At one time he had fully resolved to rush to Don Andrea, and inform him that his nephew was betraying his confidence; but a little reflection shewed him, that this would only end in the secret marriage being declared, and himself more signally defeated. On the other hand, if the bridegroom should only trip on his narrow footing, he would be rid of him for ever. Why not make him trip? How?

The grisly phantom, MURDER, flashed for a moment across his mind, and then withdrew; but with every step of the victim nearer and nearer his window, the hellish feeling returned. At last he saw immediately in front of him, on the next floor but one below him, the glossy curls of his rival's handsome head, clear in the moonlight; but as the coil of rope was in shadow, he had no notion that Ottavio was secured in any way from the frightful danger beneath him. He could resist the temptation no longer. Rising silently and swiftly from his post of observation, he seized a jug of cold water, and hurled its contents full on Ottavio's head. The shock was electric!

Coming from behind him, and, of course, wholly unexpected, with a convulsive gasp, and an irrepressible spring, the victim in an instant lost his balance, struggled vainly to catch the window-sill behind him, and then fell headlong into the gulf below.

In spite of all his self-control, a cry of delight issued from the lips of Worsley, as he exultingly beheld, the disappearance, as he thought, into the jaws of death, of the man he most hated upon earth. Immeasurable was his surprise, when, instead of hearing the dull, heavy sound on the pavement below of the mangled corpse of Ottavio, a music for which his malignant ears were throbbing, all remained comparatively still.

Stretching out to see what had happened, he perceived in the moonlight, the figure of the young Spaniard, swinging like a pendulum backwards and forwards in front of the hotel, in an apparently miraculous manner, though he was unable to tell by what means he remained suspended.

Guessing at the truth, he ground his teeth in impotent rage, and after a moment's hesitation as to what step he should take, clearly descried, on looking up, the line which stood out against the sky, showing the knots and worsted work with which it was interspersed, and which Ottavio was already beginning to use, by climbing up it with his hands, knees, and feet. In an instant Worsley rushed up to Ottavio's room, determined to cut the line, by which it was evident he was sustained, and thus insure his destruction: in addition to his previous motives for this atrocious act, was now added that of self-preservation.

If Ottavio escaped from his present peril, he would be certain to detect, and punish by the law, the man who had endeavoured to murder him. On reaching Ottavio's door, Worsley found it securely fastened on the inside. Quietly, but with all his might, he pushed against it in vain: he then tried to break in one of the panels, but they were too stoutly made to yield. He was on the point of applying his foot to kick one in, when he remembered the noise would rouse the inmates of the hotel, his rival's life be saved, and his own jeopardised by the law. Perspiration broke out in large drops on his forehead, and rolled down his face, as he stood at the door, revolving the calamitous dilemma in which his passions had involved him, yet the last thing he thought of was forbearance.

Returning to his chamber, and again looking out of his window, he perceived that Ottavio had already reached to just below the cornice. He could hear the strained line grating on the edge of the stone, as the poor young husband struggled for his life below. Worsley, in his demon-like hopes, could now trace the moonlight, shining distinctly upon the white cord, stretched quite tight from the window above to the narrow ledge below, the shadow falling vividly on the stone.

At this moment, far down in the misty depth beneath, was heard the careless song of some reveller, returning from a merry meeting, little recking the frightful tragedy impending above him. The bloodshot eyes of the Southerner were agonised with a fearful look of detection, as he heard the approaching sounds, and vainly endeavoured to pierce through the gloom of distance the figure from which they issued. In a few moments, a foot-passenger was heard to turn down a side street, and the hum of his serenade grew fainter and fainter till it was altogether lost, leaving, as before, in the gleaming moonlight, the bridegroom striving for existence, and the murderous rival thirsting for his blood.

Already Ottavio had got his left hand raised some two feet above the coping, against the edge of which one of his knees was pressed. In another second he would place a foot, and be in comparative safety. Now, if ever, appeared the moment for Worsley to annihilate him. Could he but fire his pistol at the cord and cut it? No, the line was too fine, and the noise would startle all the neighbourhood. If his pistol would not serve him, would his bowie-knife? It lay close at hand. Quick as thought, he drew the large heavy blade, and, leaning well forward to take good aim, hurled the sharp and glittering steel at the tightened life-line. At this juncture, the

Spaniard's face was turned upwards, and you might have seen an expression of hope and exultation, almost of happiness, beaming on his expressive and honest features, at having so nearly regained the dangerous cornice, when the countenance was suddenly startled into horror and amazement, as the sparkling bowie-knife struck, with a ringing sound, a few inches from his face, upon the stone, and then fell, clanging and harmless, to break in pieces on the pavement below.

The villanous act had failed, but the sharp eye of the Spaniard instantly caught sight of the protruding figure of the planter, as the moon beam fell full on the expectant visage, distorted by all the baffled passions of murder and despair. Ottavio at once recognised his foe, and the knowledge seemed to add strength and vigour to his struggles: sensible that with such an enemy thirsting for his destruction he could not extricate himself too quickly from surrounding danger. With renewed and rapid exertions he got his other knee upon the cornice, another moment he placed his foot firmly on it, and as he stood erect on his narrow way looked for an instant full in the face of his rival. What was he to do? To advance once more along the cornice directly beneath Worsley's window was, in all probability, to throw away his life; even now he hardly knew what protected him from the bullet of the would-be assassin.

One pause more his resolution was taken. Abandoning his intention of reaching his wife's apartment by the window, he drew himself up rapidly, hand over hand, into his own room, so possessed by an overwhelming determination of executing speedy vengeance on Worsley, that he thought no more of danger, neither past nor to come. Quickly casting off from his waist the leather belt by which the line was attached, and arming himself sufficiently, he drew off his shoes, unfastened his door, hastened to that of Worsley, and tried to open it, but in vain, having distinctly heard from inside the voice of the planter, trembling from agitation, uttering the words, "If you attempt to force your way in I'll shoot you dead."

Debating in his own mind what conduct he had best pursue, Ottavio leaned against the wall of his rival's room for full a quarter of an hour, uncertain what course could be selected where so many difficulties presented themselves to any action. Not a sound was audible; the idea struck Ottavio, why not seek Ivola through the apartment of her parents? He knew that Don Andrea's dread of fire obliged him to sleep with his door unsecured; in any case, he was resolved another day should not pass without boldly declaring his marriage. His present position was one he could brook no longer. If Don Andrea discovered him it would but accelerate by a few hours the discovery of their secret. This decided him; moving noiselessly down stairs, in a few seconds he reached his uncle's room, he applied his fingers to the handle of the lock; to his great joy the door yielded to his pressure, and he stood within the bedroom of his father-in-law. The next great difficulty was to close the portal without noise. As the springs of the lock were in good condition this was only a matter of time and care, and both being liberally bestowed, the task was soon accomplished, and Ottavio turned himself to pass into the room beyond.

In spite of the gravity of his situation and all the peril through which he had lately passed, Ottavio could not help laughing as he passed close to Don Andrea's head to see the loaded pistol lying on the small table beside the night light, within reach of the old man's hand, while his mouth, wide open, seemed to denote him locked in slumber. "He sleeps deeply," thought Ottavio, as he paused for a second without hearing any sound of respiration. Gliding onward, he next came to the room occupied by Donna Cattaba. She proclaimed to all the world her enjoyment of a night's rest, by the strong trumpet of repose blown at intervals of charming regularity. Another step and he stood in his wife's sanctum. In the dim light of her taper he beheld her meekly kneeling before a crucifix earnestly praying for himself.

For some minutes he remained a mute but delighted spectator, scarcely knowing how to make his presence perceptible without causing some alarm. At a slight rustle of his clothes she presently turned her head, and sprang into his arms. After their forced separation, the first since their marriage, it may easily be imagined how much they had to say to one another. Daylight dawned before they had got half through one-tenth of the subjects to be discussed between them, and most reluctantly they decided to part, having come to the resolution, at all hazards, to declare their marriage that day. Ottavio was to "bell the cat" by disclosing everything to the father.

As the young Spaniard stole back through

his uncle's room, he looked with renewed smiles at Don Andrea, still, as he supposed, fast asleep. As Ottavio's eyes rested on his sickly face the smile suddenly gave way to gravity, and gravity to alarm and awe. Not only was Don Andrea's mouth still wide open, but even his eyes were fixed and staring; the colour of his countenance and hands had become of that livid white which speaks the empire of death. So little doubt was left in Ottavio's mind, that he at once took his uncle's pulse between his fingers, and found it cold and lifeless. The invalid had probably expired almost as Ottavio was entering his chamber, and though the region of the heart was still warm beneath the clothes, it was evident his worldly struggles were at an end.

Going back to Ivola, Ottavio cautiously broke the melancholy intelligence to her, when by Ottavio's advice, she aroused her mother; and almost in the same breath communicated her own marriage, and her father's loss. As

Ottavio had foreseen, the one piece of information in the widow's mind, had a tendency to negative the other. In the very sentence in which she reproached her nephew for depriving her of her daughter, she implored his assistance under the calamity of that she determined to call her husband's fit.

At that moment, if his aunt had said his uncle was well and hearty, Ottavio would, doubtless, have endorsed the doctrine with every appearance of perfect credulity: as it was, he fell into all her views with the most amiable facility, hurried from the room, called up helps, sent for doctors, procured hot-water bottles, and did everything that could be suggested, useful or useless, till the physician arrived, and declared the cause of death to be serous apoplexy.

The genuine grief of Madame Cattaba and her child touched everybody; and the orders necessary for the occasion having been issued by Ottavio, the ladies were left to the indulgence of their sorrow, while he sought that repose his long excitement and fatigue required.

On retiring to his room, the sight of the open window and the harpoon-line recalled the attempt on his life by Worsley. He now remembered with surprise that he had not seen that amiable youth at his uncle's bedside, though several other visitors at the hotel had called to offer any services. Foreseeing much annoyance from being on terms of deadly hostility with his next-door neighbour,—pacified himself with having declared his marriage, touched by the death-bed from which he had just parted, he generously resolved to go to his rival's room, tell him what had happened, and offer him his hand.

On arriving at the lately barred and guarded door, great was his astonishment to find the portal wide open and the chamber empty—not a vestige of luggage was to be seen, the bed never seemed to have been occupied. On enquiring of the waiter, it appeared that Worsley had started at daybreak with bag and baggage, and the simple announcement that he was "going west."

"For a flying foe erect a golden bridge," thought Ottavio; and hoping that forgiveness on his part, and absence on that of his antagonist, might lead to peace and reconciliation, he hastened to his room, did justice to a comfortable breakfast, and falling asleep, never awoke till five in the afternoon.

After all the sad and inevitable formalities of the funeral were concluded, Donna Cattaba, having nothing to detain her at New York, came to the conclusion of returning home as rapidly as possible, determined to find, in the happiness of her daughter, consolation for her disappointment at a splendid match, and the loss of a somewhat querulous husband. No son-in-law could be more attentive than Ottavio,—no daughter ever was so happy as Ivola. Worsley had never returned to his house on the adjoining estate—in answer to all enquiries, he was said to have gone abroad.

A long and blissful prospect of calm enjoyment seemed opening out before the young Cattabas, and they gave themselves up to the full delight of it. Although the agricultural value of Troumaca had been greatly exhausted by previous proprietors, its romantic beauty had been sedulously cultivated. Nothing can be imagined more highly picturesque than the lakes and bowers, groves and walks with which it fringed the sea-side. After the work of the estate was done, here Ivola and Ottavio loved to wander, until day faded from the sky, discussing plans for the fairy future, and tasting in all its fulness that dream of heaven, which only pure and perfect affection can afford to man on earth.

One evening, which had passed in this blissful manner, they had watched the sun set, and the glorious moon rise, and turned to go home, when, just as they were passing up a secluded pathway from the beach, overhung by shadowy trees, they were suddenly surrounded by a party of men springing out from an ambush close by, and in defiance of every resistance made by Ottavio, carried down to the edge of the sea. On arriving at this point, one of their captors flashed some powder in a pistol, when a boat was seen to put off from a small vessel at anchor, and row to the spot.

Ottavio vainly demanded by whose authority they had been seized, and alternately threatened with vengeance or tempted with bribes those who held him and his wife prisoners. Not a word, however could he extract in reply. He then endeavoured by his cries to call some of his own people to his rescue.

This was met by an instant threat of gagging him. Knowing himself to be too far from the house to have any chance of being heard, he deemed it wisest for the present to submit, fearing that resistance might lead to still further outrage against his wife. In a few minutes they were all seated in the boat and pulling off to the vessel at anchor, which already showed signs of getting under weigh.

Scarcely had they arrived on board, and Ottavio, full of indignation, was about to demand by whose authority this villany had been committed, when Worsley, suddenly running up the after companion, appeared with a face beaming with the most malignant and baneful expression of vindictive triumph. Pointing to Ottavio he exclaimed:

"Put that fellow into irons directly."

Before the order could be executed, Ottavio, leaping, like a stag at bay, clean past the intervening men, came down on Worsley, delivering him a blow full in the right eye. In an instant the wretch was knocked down on the glass sky-light, through which he vanished into the cabin below, his blood spouting up in all directions.

"Be Gor! you've killed un," cried one of the seamen.

"I hope so," replied Ottavio, with a fervour of aspiration that put his sincerity past all question; but in another instant he himself was seized by half-a-dozen of the crew, dragged down the fore-hatch, spite of all his arguments, entreaties, and struggles, and in a few minutes both his hands and feet were securely ironed to a long bar in a dismal hold, which the solitary lanthorn showed him to be fitted as a slave deck.

"In a few minutes more, his eyes, becoming accustomed to the gloom, descried the swarthy faces of some thirty negroes, all chained with more or less security like himself. In answer to all his questions, the only reply was oaths, curses, and kicks. The fearful present, the still more frightful future appeared to his horrified imagination, like some terrific dream of Pandemonium, beneath which his sanity seemed reeling.

For a time he felt it would be impossible to

aggravate the horrors of his position, till in another instant screams in the voice of Ivola —screams in which he could hear her calling loudly and fondly on his name for assistance, pierced his soul with an agony a million times more bitter and unendurable than any pain he had yet sufiered.

Answering back her name, "Ivola, Ivola I come to you, I come to you," he exerted himself with frantic strength to tear off his fetters, but in vain.

The screams presently died away; the ship began tossing to a heavy sea. She was already under canvass, bearing him away from his home and people, from all who could assist his wife or him, and to what fate?"

"Better I had never been born!" thought poor Ottavio, and overpowered by frenzy and despair, insensibility mercifully extended her shield over him, and he lost all consciousness.

When he next revived, he found himself lying on the deck of what was evidently the chief cabin, still chained but not in the painful posture he had before occupied. Standing beside him was Worsley, hideously gashed in all directions by the glass through which he had fallen, while his head was strapped and plaistered, and still bedaubed with blood.

"Listen to me, you scoundrel," said he, shaking his fist as he kicked the fettered body of his rival. "I have sent for you that you may thoroughly understand the revenge I am resolved to enjoy at your expense. You are now a prisoner on board my slave ship. I am now sailing to Cuba, to complete my cargo. In a few days I shall have three hundred and fifty slaves on board. I shall then run you all down South, and sell you with the rest of them, while your wife I shall keep with me."

Commanding himself to be calm as much as possible, Ottavio simply asked: "Where is my wife?" when instantly, to his inexpressible relief, a faint voice replied:

"Here I am, Ottavio, unharmed except by

grief for you. I will die a thousand deaths before you shall regret my existence."

"Silence, Madam," interposed Worsley.

"Your wife, fellow, as you hear, is in my state-room, from which she shall only pass to be sold hereafter for a slave like you. There is no indignity that human being can undergo to which you shall not both be subjected by my ——;" the sound was yet trembling on his lips, when a mighty, yet indescribable noise, swallowing up all before it, seemed to shake the whole cabin—the strong oak beam above Worsley's head splintered into a thousand fragments, while the arm that he had been shaking in anticipated vengeance over the prostrate form of Ottavio, was pierced through and through by a long oak splinter, that beating it down and penetrating also the muscles of his back, pinned it to his side with an amount of pain that seemed appalling.

At this moment the distant boom of a heavy gun was borne down to their ears by the rising gale, and the following moment the voice of the officer of the watch called down the companion: "A man of war steamer firing on the weather-beam."

"All hands make sail," answered Worsley, in a voice faint with excessive pain, and making an effort to reach the companion ladder. But the effort was too much for him. Some inarticulate words escaped him, and groaning heavily he fell along the deck at Ottavio's feet. At this juncture a rushing sound was heard.

"Be gor! Jim," said a seaman coming down into the cabin, "that shot is letting in the water and no mistake."

Ottavio turned his eyes at these words and perceived that the shot which had so seriously wounded Worsley, had struck the slaver below the water line. Being a thirty-two-pounder the hole thus made in the ship's side was one of considerable size, and the briny element poured through it like a sluice. After penetrating the side the shot had struck one of the chief beams lengthwise, splitting it up athwartships, and scattering its sharp long splinters in all directions. What between the steamer chasing them and now firing guns in quick succession—the necessity for stopping the leaks that followed the shot holes, and the insensibility of their owner; his severe wound, and the absence of any surgeon, the Yankee Captain had so much on his hands that he seemed half-distracted. In vain he followed the last injunction of Worsley, and crowded sail upon sail. Canvass was no match for steam; and while Worsley was uttering frightful yells of pain as the seamen vainly endeavoured to drag out of his flesh the jagged oak-splinter, Ottavio, with the utmost thankfulness heard a stern voice hailing through a trumpet in French—"Shorten all sail and come under our lee or I'll sink you." Then followed in the Yankee Captain's voice a volley of oaths and curses, and a noise as if some of the crew, taking the matter into their own hands, had cut séveral of the halliards and let all go by the run. Then came fresh curses and the flapping of the loosened canvass in the wind, in the midst of which Ottavio heard a boat run along the lee side of the slaver, and the jumping on board of several men.

His suspense did not endure much longer. He soon saw the glitter of a French uniform on the cabin steps, and waiting till he perceived the officer's face, called to him for assistance, and in a few forcible words narrated the villany of which his wife and himself had been made the victims. Nothing could exceed the kindness and attention of the French Commander and his officers. If Ottavio and Ivola had been his own children he could not have shewn them more tenderness. Having taken possession of his prize and freed the unhappy slaves, he removed to the French Steam Corvette *La Sylphide*, Ottavio and his bride, and Worsley as a prisoner; though the latter, too ill to be questioned, was put under the care of the Surgeon. A prize crew and master, were then put on board the Slaver, and the French Steamer at once made all way back to the bay where Ottavio had been kidnapped. Landing them there in safety and thankfulness on the following morning, they carried off to sea, as a prisoner, Worsley, for future trial as a pirate, a doom which though fully merited, he, nevertheless, escaped—lockjaw following on his wounds a few days afterwards.

When Ottavio heard this result his relief was great and complete. His bride soon recovered the terrible alarm she had undergone and the commander of La Sylphide, from whom this narrative came, receives frequently from Troumaca a handsome present of Southern produce, to remind him of the great obligation he conferred by the timely capture and the kindness of his rescue.

"And is that all, sir?" remarked Captain

McCrotchet, thinking to put Scrapegrace out of countenance when his tale was ended.

"Far from it, Captain McCrotchet," quickly replied Scapegrace. "Ivola presented Ottavio with twins two years running, and they were all the picture of their father."

"Ah! sir," said McCrotchet," "if the fine bairns grow up with only half your impudence they'll puzzle the gude man their father vera sadly. And now, gentlemen, if ye'll give me a dish of tea, I'll make for the shore, and wish ye a good evening."

About eight o'clock the Captain rose from the ward-room table, and all the officers rose at the same time.

He was then sent on shore in one of the ship's gigs, and the same opportunity was taken by Julius to seek his hammock and get to bed in early time, as he had to keep the middle watch, and would, therefore, be called at midnight to rise and go on deck, and there pace up and down till four o'clock on the following morning—this weary vigil only enlivened by the chiming of the ship's bells in the different parts of the harbour, the cry of the Sentries—"All's well," and an occasional shower of rain to make the quarter-deck more wretched and slippery.

As soon as the officers resumed their seats on the Captain's departure, and the first lieutenant returned from seeing him off deck, they began, of course, to canvass their Superior.

"Well, Heathfield, did not I tell you now exactly the sort of chap he would turn out—there he is to a very hair."

"Yes, you did certainly; but, however, he does not seem such a bad sort of fellow as I should have imagined from the description of young Scapegrace."

"By the way, what an impudent young varlet that youngster is. I thought at first he was going to blurt out before the Captain's face, word for word what his father had said of him."

"I will tell you what, Heathfield," said McMurdo, "you may depend upon it that young fellow has got his brains placed in the right quarter. I never saw anything done more readily in my life than the way he turned it off at last, after putting us all in a most mortal fright."

"Yes," said the marine officer, "I was almost ready to have gone down into my boots. Let me see, how was it—what was it he said?"

"Why," said McMurdo, "instead of telling the Captain his father had said he had sixty good reasons for never obliging anybody, he converted it into sixty good reasons for taking up a position of strong defence. Of course a fellow who never obliges anybody must be perfectly unassailable, and, what is more, I have no doubt we shall find him a perfect hedgehog as soon as he gets his pennant up and puts his gold-lace toggery on."

"Well, I do not augur of him so badly as that. If he only sticks to his text about doing what other people think about, and carries that out upon the Russians with as smart a ship as this Sancebox might be made, depend upon it, we shall all of us see a little prize money, and many of us get our promotion."

"And many more of us knocked on the head," said McMurdo. "So as this is the general conclusion of Her Majesty's service, just shove the grog bottle this way."

At nine o'clock on the following morning, the wardroom gig was sent ashore to the steps which the Captain had named; and there, not only punctual to the minute but a few minutes before-hand, was seen Captain Mc Crotchet, standing, in full dress toggery, with his clerk behind him, ready to step into the boat and be rowed on board.

This punctuality was not lost on any of the beholders.

"I say, Jim," said the Coxswain to the Stroke-oar, as the Captain went up the side, "our new Skipper is a little before his time rather than after. You see if he does not stir the lazy hands up. Depend upon it, they will catch a tartar in him."

"Sarve 'em right," said the Stroke-oar. "I think it is one of the best things going in a ship, to have a Skipper who will keep the skulkers to their work, and then the smart hands have not got to do all the duty, as they have in your lubberly, disorderly ships, where the Skipper is always afraid to exert his authority."

"Ah! there won't be much fear of that here, I think."

"So much the better," the other said.

"Well, we shall see." And the boat's crew running up the ship's side, the gig was dropped astern in charge of one of the ships boys.

As soon as Captain McCrochet touched the quarter-deck, the pennant, which had been previously hauled down, was hoisted again. The hands were mustered on the quarter-deck.

The gallant officer read his commission; and then, calling the crew around the capstan, uttered these words:

"My men, I am happy to tell you, I hear a very good account of your discipline and conduct from the first Lieutenant. You will understand that it is my rule to make every man do his duty. I never overlook offences, for I think it spoils the discipline of a ship. I always do what I can to reward good men; and when I see a man doing his duty, I always keep a memorandum in my mind for that man's benefit. In the war which is coming with Russia, I hope the Saucebox and her crew will be well-known and long-remembered; and it shall not be my fault, if I do not give you many an opportunity of distinguishing yourselves, and making a little prize money. All I can promise you, therefore, is, that if you do your duty well, whenever the service will allow me the opportunity, you will find me always ready to care for your interest, and to oblige you with any indulgence and comfort in my power; but, remember, I will not stand any drunkenness—I will not stand any slack discipline—everything must be sharp and out of hand; and if any man feels he is not up to the mark in my ship, the sooner he makes himself scarce the better. Boatswain's mate, pipe down."

The Officers lingered round the capstan for a few minutes after the men were piped down, and thus gave an opportunity to Captain McCrotchet to turn round to them and say:—

"Gentlemen, I am much pleased to make your acquaintance. From what I have said to the crew you will gather, that you have only to do your duty zealously, and no one will be so delighted to promote your comfort as myself."

The Captain then bowed to his officers, and marched into his cabin.

This charming little indication of his benevolent character produced a great effect upon his assembled officers.

"I say, I suppose by that allusion to our comfort," said the Paymaster, "the Skipper intends to stand some leave for us before the ship sails."

"Well, I do not know," said McMurdo, "I have not much fancy for men praising themselves."

"Ah, Mac, you are so censorious, you know. At any rate I shall go and ask him for leave. I just want to run up and see my old mother, who lives at Richmond, and when once a ship is going out on war service, one never knows who is to come back."

"Well, you come back," said McMurdo, "and tell us what he says; although I suppose he must let you go, because all your stores are on board, are they not?"

"Yes, all."

"Well, you have got your clerk on board. I do not know what you can be wanted to do.

I do not see how he can refuse your leave well."

"No certainly not," said the Paymaster, and going down to the main deck, he sent his compliments and his name to the Captain, by the Captain's clerk, and begged he would be kind enough to spare him a few minutes to see him.

"The Captain will see you, sir," said the Clerk, and in went the Paymaster.

"What can I do for you, Mr. Weighdip?"

"Why, thank you, Captain McCrotchet, as the ship is leaving England on serious service I shall be very glad of three days' leave, just to run up to Richmond and say good bye to my mother, who is advanced in life, and I may not have an opportunity of seeing her again!"

"My dear sir," said the Captain, "I am extremely sorry, but the fact is, you see, the Paymaster's services on board are so very light that I feel a delicacy in giving you leave of absence at this particular time. In point of fact, you may say, you know, that your services take you ashore every day, you know."

"Still, Captain, I have had no opportunity of going away to—"

"Yes, but you see your services are so very light, they naturally involve a great deal of time ashore. I am very sorry I must refuse you. I must decline this, Mr. Weighdip."

"I hope you will be able to re-consider your decision, Captain McCrotchet."

"Impossible, Mr. Weighdip, impossible! I never re-consider a decision. If you had been suffering under an arduous discharge of duty, you know, or any case of that sort, it would have been a different thing, you know; but really the Paymaster has so little to do—all your stores come on board with so little trouble, and you have the assistance of the Admiralty Clerk. It is quite impossible. I am very sorry. Good morning;" and Captain McCrotchet bowed the poor Paymaster out of the cabin.

Swearing and vowing vengeance on the head of his Captain, poor Weighdip descended to the wardroom.

"Well, Weighdip, my boy, what success?"

"No go," growled Weighdip.

"Why?" said McMurdo.

"The most absurd reason in the world. I am not to go up and bid adieu to my family, because my duties as Paymaster on board a ship are so light, and, if I had been doing heavy duty, he might have taken it into consideration."

"The deuce he does!" said the first Lieutenant, who had been reading a letter. "Egad, that is my very case. I have been worked to death here. By Jove! I will go up and ask for two or three days' leave while he is in that humour."

"I wish you may get it," slyly said Mc Murdo.

But paying no attention to this hint, away sprang the first Lieutenant, sent in the sentry to ask if the Captain was at liberty, and receiving permission to enter, immediately availed himself of the authority.

"What can I do for you, Mr. Heathfield?" said McCrotchet, with a gracious smile.

"Why, Captain McCrotchet, I wish, as we are going to sea on war service—I wish to take an early opportunity of mentioning to you that I have been fagging on board the ship night and day ever since I first hoisted the Queen's pennant on her. I have completed all the rigging of the ship,; my second lieutenant has had some leave, and now he is on board; he is a very able officer, and I should be extremely obliged to you if you would grant me a few days' leave to go and see my family."

"Well, really, my dear Mr. Heathfield," said the Captain, "it would give me the greatest pleasure in the world to do so; but what can I do? The situation of first lieutenant is of so very responsible a nature; there is so very much to do, in fact, he is the whole Alpha and Omega of the ship's routine. You must see, that it is quite impossible for me to spare the first lieutenant in the midst of fitting out."

"Well, but sir, just consider the hard work I have had to go through."

"O! precisely, it is that vera hard work that is the glory of the first Lieutenant. It is the post of honor and authority: in fact, you know that is the very reason why I am very sorry to refuse you your leave. It is impossible to permit the first Lieutenant to leave. Why, you know he has all the work of the ship in his hands."

"I hope, sir, you will reconsider your decision."

"O! no, sir, that is one of the rules of my life. I never reconsider a decision. Once decided, there is no appeal. Good morning."

The first Lieutenant made his superior officer a stiff bow, and got out of the cabin as quickly as possible.

"Well, Heathfield," said McMurdo, "what luck?"

"Luck! Luck! Luck be hanged! When I go and ask that fellow a favor again—ahem!—that is all. Ah! well. Here, doctor, you had better go up and try him, and see what you can make of him."

"Catch a weasel asleep!" said the Doctor.

"What is the meaning of all this?" said the Marine Officer.

"Why the meaning of it is, that we all want a little leave before the ship goes to sea, and here have I been working like a slave ever since the pennant was first hoisted. I have got all my work nearly completed. I gave the second Lieutenant under me as much leave as he wanted; and now, when my superior officer comes on board, I am not allowed to have any leave forsooth at all, because my work is so heavy."

"And I," said the Purser, "I am refused leave, because my work is so light. How I hate such inconsistency!"

"Ah! ha! indeed!" said the Marine Officer. "Well, then, I think I can go up, and tease him for a little leave. He cannot say my work is heavy, and he cannot say my work is light."

"Well, go and try, Mr. Myrtle."

"Aye, Myrtle," said McMurdo. "You military men, you know, you can deal better with superior officers than we can. You are accustomed to mess ashore, all on an equality. I dare say you can manage him better than anybody else."

"Ah! yes. Just so. I will just go and give him a spell." And Lieutenant Myrtle accordingly adjusted his stock, and sent in his name to the Captain, who in due course received him.

"Good morning, Mr. Myrtle," said the Captain with his usual smile. "How do you do? A very fine set of men your draft of marines seems to be on board here."

"Yes, Captain McCrotchet, they are a very fine set of men. I have taken considerable pains with them, and got them into very good order, seeing the short time they have been in the ship. They are very willing, and make themselves useful to the blue jackets; and I am in hopes that, as soon as I show them the enemy, they will do every justice to the Russians."

"I think so too—I think so too—they reflect great credit on you."

"I am glad you think so, Captain McCrotchet, for my family live down in Cornwall, and we are going on what may be a last cruise to many of us. I want to know whether you can oblige me with a week's leave?"

"A week's leave, Mr. Myrtle? Well, certainly, that is a very modest request for you to make, as the ship is under orders to get to sea, as quickly as possible. You certainly might have asked for a fortnight."

"O! thank you, Captain McCrotchet. I am obliged to you, but I will not take more than a week, and I am very thankful to you for granting it to me"—going out of the cabin at quick march.

"Stop, stop, Mr. Myrtle: you mistake," said the Captain. "I did not mean to say that I granted you the leave—it is impossible to do that."

"Impossible, Captain McCrotchet? I am doing nothing on board at present. I have got my men in excellent order, and my sergeant knows his duty. Of course, I have nothing to do with the fitting out of the ship. At present there is really no call for my services."

"O! I beg your pardon, Mr. Myrtle: you do yourself a great injustice. If there had been two officers of marines on board, it would have given me the greatest possible pleasure to spare one of them; but as you see you are the only officer of marines on board, it would be quite inconvenient, and indeed it is not possible, to spare you out of the ship for a week."

"Well, Captain McCrotchet, suppose we say four days. I could not possibly go down to Cornwall and back in less than four days."

"O! precisely—I know that. It is not the length of time I look at, because I am quite aware that you could not do less in going to Cornwall than a week; but as you see, you are the only marine officer. It is a totally different principle—I must not spare you at all; and, as to your not being of any use on board at present, you must not do yourself that great injustice. You know, Mr. Myrtle, that when marines join from the land, and come in contact with seamen, very often little jealousies arise between the two classes; and, in case of any disturbance between the seamen and marines, your appearance would be invaluable. I could not possibly think of sparing you. Any one but the marine-officer could go, you know, because, in point of fact, the marine-officer is the only officer on board the ship, for whom we have no substitute as it were. Sorry to disappoint, you know; but the opportunities of writing by the post are now so excellent, and so ample, that really you must be content with the opportunity of taking leave of your friends by letter. Good morning, Mr. Myrtle." And the Captain looked down at his writing paper, as much as to say, take yourself off, Mr. Myrtle, with all expedition.

Poor Myrtle drew himself up with amazing military stiffness, but not being over redundant in ideas, nothing suggested itself to him to alter his Captain's determination, and, after a second or two's pause, Myrtle turned to the right about face, and stalked out of the cabin, bursting with rage.

When he came down to the wardroom, and repeated his modest request, there was a general roar at his expense.

"Holloa, Myrtle, why what the deuce could

induce you to think you could get leave when the first lieutenant was refused?"

"It is a shame—it is a great shame," said Myrtle.

"I like that," said the first lieutenant. "A fellow like you—a jolly marine who comes on board here, and have had all your time to yourself, and, until the ship is paid off will never have to keep a single watch. Hang it, my dear fellow, if any one can do without leave you can."

"It is a shame; it is a great shame," said Myrtle, and, seeing he could get no compassion in the wardroom, he indignantly left its authoritative precincts and took himself off to the midshipman's mess, where, being a very young man himself, he often liked to go and have a little chat and a glass of grog with one or two of the older midshipmen.

"I say, Smith, my boy, give me a glass of grog," said he, entering into the midshipman's mess. "Let us drink confusion to this confounded prig of a fellow who has just come on board."

"Holloa, what is the matter, Mr. Myrtle?" said one or two of the midshipmen.

"Well, what do you think? Here have I been on board getting my men in order ever since the ship has been commissioned, and now I want to go down to Cornwall, just to say good bye to my family, and this Skipper of ours, who has just come on board, says I cannot have leave."

"Why, are we going to sail directly?"

"O! no. As I understand the ship is not going to sail for a fortnight."

"What is the reason then?"

"Why, was there ever anything so preposterous?—because, he says I am the only officer of marines on board, and he cannot supply my place if anything arises."

"Oh!" said the senior midshipman, "if that is the reason, I will go and ask him for leave. He cannot say that of me; there are plenty of us to supply one another's places."

"Ah! yes; do go up and ask him leave. I should like to see now, what he would say to that case."

"Oh! by Jove, I will soon try him. Let me take a glass of grog first, to get my courage up. Here, steward, bring us the rum and cold water directly, and a few glasses."

"Aye, aye! sir," said the steward, and forthwith that delectable spirit made its appearance in a quart decanter, with a large blue jug, the lip of it broken off, and charged with some very questionable looking fluid.

"Dear me," said the marine officer, "this water of yours looks a very queer colour. You do not filter it, do you?"

"Oh, no," said Smith, "we do not trouble ourselves with a filter in the midshipman's mess. As to the colour of the water, I do not think it is more than a little rust."

"Aye, perhaps the pump hose is new, and there is some of the tar come off it."

"Nay, mon," said the Scotch second-master, "it is no tar, but ye see the water must be pumped from the hold through a hose, and it is impossible at first, in a new hose not to have the water a little dirty or so, but it doesna' do to be too nice."

"Put a little more rum in it, and you will soon forget the dirt," said the mate. "We have ordered a good stock of wine into the mess; but it will not be on board till next week, and as soon as we get a little more in kelter, we shall be able to treat you better—your health, Mr. Myrtle," and Smith tossed off his stiff glass of rum and water. "Now," said he, I am ready for the Skipper. I will come down, my boys, and let you know what he says in a minute."

Away went Mr. Smith, and sent in his name by the sentry, and received permission to advance into the penetralia of the cabin.

"Good morning, youngster," said Captain McCrotchet, with an unusual urbanity. "Is there any little matter that I can do for you?"

"Please, sir, I am very anxious to go home and see my friends before the ship sails, sir, for the Mediterranean, if you will be kind enough to grant me eight and forty hours' leave."

"Eight and forty hours' leave, Mr. Smith, do you know what you are asking?"

"Well, sir, I hope not a favour too great for your kindness."

"Just consider yourself, Mr. Smith. On board this ship there are something like sixteen midshipmen, counting all youngsters. Supposing I were to grant eight and forty hours' leave to every youngster who asked, it, where do you think the duties of the ship would be?"

"Of course, Captain McCrotchet, that would never do; but I believe very few of the midshipmen will ask this favour at your hands. My parents are far advanced in life, and if I do not see them before the ship sails, perhaps I shall never see them again."

"It is very excellent of you, Mr. Smith, to honour your father and your mother, but you must remember, you know, you have now entered the Queen's service. That is the only measure of propriety for us all. I cannot grant to one midshipman what I do not to another, unless there is some special claim upon me to take it out of the general case, and, as I said before, if I were to grant every midshipman eight and forty hours' leave, I should have every one out of the ship, and nothing done. It is impossible—quite impossible. There is nothing special in your case, for all have fathers and mothers to visit probably. I cannot do it—good morning."

Poor Smith immediately backed water, and got down to his midshipman's berth with as little delay as possible.

"Well," said Myrtle, "what success?"

"Oh! bless his little grey eyes," said Smith. "Success! as much success as if I had been trying to put salt on the tail of one of mother Carey's chickens."

"Upon what ground has he refused you? He could not say you were the only officer in the ship of your class."

"No, by Jove, he came down upon me just exactly on the opposite tack. He would not grant me any leave because he said there were sixteen of us midshipmen altogether, and if he granted leave to one he ought to grant it to all—that then we should all be out of the ship and no duty done—that he could not possibly think of granting leave to any midshipman, unless his was a special case."

"Oh! I see what he means," said Julius Scapegrace, "he must have had me in his eye."

"How the deuce should he have you in his eye?"

"Oh! because mine is a special case. He and my poor old governor, who is dead, were special friends at the club. I will just run up and ask him leave. I do not stand in any of your way, you know."

"Oh! you do not stand in our way. Just go up and have a shy at him; the more the merrier. He must grant leave to some of us presently."

"Well, faint heart never won fair lady—here goes," said Julius. "Just give me a brush first, to see if I am all tidy."

And young Scapegrace stood up while another of his brother midshipmen passed a whisk over his clothes; he then drew a pocket comb through his hair, and off he flew up the ladder to charge the imperturbable Mc Crotchet.

He, like his predecessor, Smith, sent in his name by the sentry, and, like Smith, he received leave to enter.

"Ah! how do you do, Mr. Scapegrace," said McCrotchet, with that politeness so unusual in post captains. "Is there anything I can do for you?"

"Well, you are very kind, Captain McCrotchet," said Julius. "You were kind enough to ask after my sisters last evening, sir, and I explained to you that we were all left alone in the world by the death of my poor father, who had the pleasure of knowing you, and, before I go to the Mediterranean, it would be a great comfort to me to go up and take a final leave of my sisters, if you would be kind enough to grant me a few days' leave."

"A day or two's leave, Mr. Julius. Ah! that is a very serious affair. You see, if you and I had been perfect strangers, you know, and I had not the pleasure of knowing your father, it would be another thing; but as the case stands, do you see, if I were to grant you leave it would be felt as a sort of injustice by your brother midshipmen, when they saw the Captain make a private favouritism, as it were, in granting leave to one youngster in particular, merely because he happened to be acquainted with the youngster's father."

"O! sir, I do not think they would look upon it in that light."

"Pardon me, Mr. Scapegrace: you are young in the service—very young—a mere child. When you come to my time of life, you will be better able to judge how things are looked at and regarded. The thing is quite impossible. Nothing is so necessary for superior officers as to be quite impartial. If you were a stranger to me I might have listened to your request—as it is now, you know, it is quite out of the question. Good morning."

Poor Julius turned round on his heel, and retraced his steps.

"Holloa! little Scrappy, you are very much down in the mouth," chorussed the rest of the middies.

"Why, has he refused you?" said another.

"Tell us all about it," said a fourth.

"Why, he says that he might perhaps have granted me leave, if he had not happened to know my father; but he cannot possibly give me leave now, because it would look like a piece of partial friendship."

"Ha! ha! sir," said the youngsters, laughing.

"It appears to me, sir," said the Assistant Surgeon, who, like his chief, was a Scotchman, "that Captain McCrotchet is a vera sensible, discreet, well-comported gentleman; and I think nothing is more consistent than his conduct: he canna let the whole berth go very properly, so he refused Mr. Smith. He canna let an only officer go, so, with great pain nae doubt, he was compelled to refuse Lieutenant Myrtle. He canna give way to the whisperings of private friendship, and therefore he could not let Mr. Scapegrace go; but, mark ye, a gentleman like myself, mon, is the special case he points out. The only relation I have in the world is just dead, and here is a note for the funeral. He canna refuse me on a point of duty, because there is a surgeon to do all that is necessary to the sick list. The giving me leave will no impose upon him the necessity for doing so to any others. I am a total stranger to him, and therefore friendship will not stand in the way. It is quite clear, therefore, that he just means me to go up and ask leave for mysel, though he has never expressed it."

"Aha! Sawney—well done, Sawney!" cried two or three of the youngsters.

"I tell you what it is, boys, if ye ca' me Sawney, I will rap you over the sconce," said the Assistant Surgeon, taking down a rule from his desk.

"Well, Mr. McLynn, you had better go up and ask him," said the Marine Officer.

"That is just what I am going to do," said McLynn; and putting his rule in its place, and adjusting his hair, and smoothing his coat, he stalked up to the Captain.

Having sent in his name and been admitted, the same quiet smile received him. "Good morning, Mr. McLynn: I am happy to see you. What can I do for you?"

"Nae great muckle thing, sir," said McLynn. "I hae just received this circular, Captain McCrotchet, and the only relation I had is now lying above ground, waiting to be buried; and if you would be kind enough to grant me a short amount of leave, I would just go and pay my last respects to the deceased."

"O! Mr. McLynn," said the Captain, "I am very sorry indeed, that you should have such a mournful occasion to leave the ship; but you see, we do not know exactly when our orders to sail will come. We are going, you know, into the midst of war, Mr. McLynn. We may soon have to bury one another. As your relative is dead, you know it cannot assuage her feelings to see you. Her will is made too, and your going or staying cannot affect that you know. Besides I should be very sorry, just as we are going out to scenes of death and danger, that your spirits should be depressed by travelling a long journey to a family funeral: it is always a melancholy duty, and if we can avoid it on good ground or reason, it is a piece of wisdom to do so."

"Well, sir, a good deal depends upon circumstances. As to my poor Aunt, just deceased, I received a great deal of kindness from her, and if I were going to die myself to-morrow, it would be a consolation to know, that I had shown a last respect to her remains."

"Ah! excellent, Mr. McLynn. Very good indeed. It shows the high sense of duty you entertain; but you know, Mr. Mc Lynn, there are public duties as well as private duties, and your duties to the sick of the ship—"

"Preceesely, Captain McCrotchet: they have all been admirably cared for. The sick list is reduced to a mere nominal figure, and my excellent chief, Mr. McMurdo, will, I am sure, raise no obstacle to my receiving this kindness at your hands."

"That is very possibly so, Mr. McLynn. But you see, granting leave is a very awkward thing when a ship is going abroad, and you must remember, Mr. McLynn, though I have no doubt as to your merits as an officer, that you are an entire stranger to me. If I had had the honour of being acquainted with you or your family before joining your ship, that might have been some ground for my stretching a little the rules of discipline, but where an officer applies to me for a favour, who was a perfect stranger to me up to the time of the application, of course you can but be well aware there is but one rule for my conduct—that is, simply the good of the service; and, therefore, I refuse you this application, Mr. McLynn, with great regret, but not the slightest hesitation—good morning."

McLynn stood up for a minute with his mouth wide open.

"I need not detain you any longer in the cabin," said the Captain, looking up.

"Thank you, sir," said McLynn, very sheepishly: turning round, he walked out of the cabin, and without uttering a word took his seat once more in the midshipmen's berth.

"Holloa, Mac the second," said Smith, "yours does not seem such a clear case then, after all as you thought when you started."

"He is just the most incomprehensible mon I ever had to deal with in the whole course of my life."

"On what grounds has he refused you, Doctor?" inquired the marine officer.

"Precisely the reverse of those on which he refused Mr. Scapegrace. He cannot grant me leave because I am a perfect stranger to him, he says."

"O! capital, capital," said the midshipmen.

"I tell you what it is," said the marine officer; "there was some one dining at the Wardroom table yesterday who said that this fellow, at the club in London, had the established character of always having sixty good reasons for never doing a kindness to anyone. Hang me if he is not quite right, whoever it was said it.

"I said that," cried Julius. "It was my father who gave him that character. I never thought of it when I went up to ask him leave; but hang me if my governor was not right to a 't.'"

"A pleasant fellow to live under," growled one or two of the other midshipmen.

At this time there was a pipe heard in the ship. "Sideboys, Sideboys," and then one of the ship's boys came running down: "Please, sir, the Captain's clerk is to go ashore with the Captain."

"He is not here," said the midshipmen.

"O! this precious Captain is going on shore. What is he going on shore about?"

"There goes the first Lieutenant rushing up on deck."

"I will go up and see," said the marine officer.

"So will I," said Smith.

"Hang me if I will," said the Scotch Assistant Surgeon.

When the other officers had reached the deck, Captain McCrochet was found walking up and down, waiting until the wardroom gig was ready and the sideboys were over the side.

As soon as this was done, the midshipman of the Watch came to report it to the first Lieutenant; the first Lieutenant reported it to the captain.

"O! by the way, Mr. Heathfield," said the Captain, turning round to the first Lieutenant, "I will send you a note on board this afternoon, with instructions as to what I want done to my cabin; and I shall give myself leave of absence from the ship for the next few days; and, until I return, get on as fast as you can with whatever is to be done."

The first Lieutenant muttered something, and made a stiff bow.

The other officers all gathered round the gangway, and away went Captain McCrotchet, having refused to every one a favour he might easily have granted, and having granted to himself the favour he had sixty good reasons for refusing to every one else.

CHAPTER VIII.

Our story now takes us back to the Nonsuch Regiment.

The order for the route had arrived; and the following morning, at day-break, parade was ordered, that the officers and men might fall in, and commence their march to Portsmouth.

"Montagu had left mess on the night before at an early hour, in order to retire to bed; and by early rest, prepare himself for the next day's toil and early rising. He had previously to this been up to London several times, and ordered from his outfitter every article that he thought he could possibly want for a campaign in the Crimea, the regiment having been ordered to Sebastopol.

Just as he had given his last directions to his servant, and was taking off his uniform to retire for the night, a tap came to his door; and, having given the word, "Come in," the door opened, and in walked Spinney.

"I say, Montagu," said Spinney, "have you heard the lark that is afloat?"

"No," said Montagu, "I have not. What is it?"

"Ever since that court-martial business, the regiment has been remarkably free from larks, and every thing else in the way of amusement. Well, the story is, that Worsted has been refused to-day by the old Attorney's ward, Miss Wyndham."

"Has he indeed? He always used to express himself so certain, that he only had to make an offer in order to get her. From whom has come the intelligence that he was refused?"

"Never mind," said Spinney, "who my informant was—there is the fact."

"Is it possible? How it must have astonished Worsted! I do not believe for a moment that he supposed such a thing was possible."

"Well, but that is not all. It seems that the cunning old dog, Doem, had previously taken a judgment for £300, and Worsted rather looked to the marriage to help him out with the tin. He had scarcely, however, got refused by Miss Wyndham, when in came a dunning letter from Doem, demanding the money.. This Worsted has not been able at all to raise, and I am told that Doem has issued process against him, to take him into custody before the regiment leaves the Town. The question is, what the deuce will Worsted do? He is kept on the tenter hooks of suspense all to-night; and to-morrow the chances are, that, instead of going abroad with the regiment, he will be locked up in quod. Is it not a lark?"

"Well," said Montagu, "it certainly is not without its laughable features; but I must say I pity the unfortunate Worsted, to have fallen into such hands."

"Well, pity is all very well in its way, but as we have had our laugh at him, I must tell you that Walduck has come to me quietly, under the rose, to see if he can get Worsted out of this bother."

"How?" said our hero.

"Well," said Spinney, "I will tell you how Walduck proposes to do it. You see to-night Worsted might get clear of the regiment easy enough, and no doubt double this fellow with the writ."

"Well, but how is he to be at early parade, at daylight to-morrow morning, in order to march?"

"Yes, precisely," said Spinney; "that

makes the whole difficulty of the case. The officer of the law is sure to be on the watch all the night; and, though he might be foiled in the dark, yet, when daylight came, I do not see how it is possible for Worsted to dodge him; and once in the officer's hands, I am told, all chance of escape ceases—he will be taken off to prison; and if his friends cannot pay the debt, he will be in prison some time, and have to pass through the Insolvent Court."

"Upon my word, Captain Spinney, this is a very serious thing for him."

"Oh, indeed it is," said Spinney; "but, however, he has chosen to put his foot into this mess, and he must take the racket of it. What could induce the fellow to accept accommodation from a man of Doem's character. You, I suppose, Montagu, have not been silly enough to leave any of your papers in Mr. Doem's hands?"

"Thank you, Captain Spinney; but I never

had any paper of that sort to leave, and I never intend to have any; and so of course it is neither in Mr. Doem's hands nor in anybody else's hands," and at the same time our hero thought with a twinge, upon the price he had paid for several articles, which, though paid in ready money, did not the less diminish the means of the purchaser. "Are there no means of our helping Worsted in this pinch?"

"Well, I think there are," said Spinney.

"How is it to be done?"

"Well, Walduck has got some scheme in his head. I do not know I am sure whether it will succeed; but as I am the first captain for purchase, I do not choose to have anything to do with it. It is a little too full of risk for me, if this matter should come out before a court-martial."

At this moment a footstep was heard upon the stair.

"Ah!" said Spinney—"there is Walduck. I will wish you good evening," and away bolted Spinney; but Montagu could hear the two meet on the staircase, and the Captain say—

"I have prepared him for it, and I think he will do it."

"All right," said Walduck, entering our hero's room without knocking, and closing the door after him.

"Montagu, my boy," said Walduck. "you heard from Spinney the fix that poor Worsted is in. I am sure you will agree with me that every man ought to do an unjust extortioner if possible, especially that extortioner being old Doem."

"Well, let us hear your plan, and I will tell you whether I will do anything."

"It is simply this—we have parade ordered for day-break to-morrow, to begin the march to Portsmouth. Now we have information that these infernal bums will be on the look out close to Worsted's quarters, to pounce upon him as he goes to parade. I think, therefore, that if some one were to sleep in Worsted's quarters, other than Worsted, and were to pass out in the morning as if going to parade, the sheriff's officers would pounce upon him; and while busy discussing with him the question of his identity, Worsted could slip off quietly, fall in at parade and start."

"Well, but then what an awkward position it will be for the poor devil who is seized by the officers: he will be late on parade, and get a wagging in that way. How will he be able to persuade the Israelite that he is not the right man?"

"Oh! that is easy enough; because, in the grey of the morning the sheriff's officer will not be able to distinguish identity much; but when he is appealed to, and shown that he has got hold of an ensign instead of a captain, and that Worsted is nearly old enough to be your father, he will let go the wrong prey, because the man who makes a mistake in his capture is liable to a serious action; and then, when the Israelite hastens to parade, he will scarcely dare to take Worsted out of the ranks; and, dressed up in his uniform like the rest of us, he will hardly know him even when he sees him."

"But what is all this to me?" said Montagu. "If Captain Worsted gets into any scrapes, why does he not get out of them?"

"Well, the fact is, Montagu, my boy, you might do us a good turn in this matter. You are the youngest man in the regiment, you can afford to be a little larky; and if you will sleep to-night in Worsted's quarters, and let the sheriff capture you as you go out to-morrow to parade, it will be taken as a very great kindness."

"This is rather a serious matter; but if you pledge your word that I shall be asked to do nothing more, I do not care if I embark in it. If the debt were to any one else I would not interfere, but being to old Doem, I think certainly it is a fair retribution upon him; and if he can be left to write this off as a bad debt, it will not only do him good but—"

"Oh! never mind the good done to Doem. We will pass that over. I think he is a little past anything of that sort: though it will be a fine lark against him at any rate; and now, as you consent, I will tell you the course of action. Come to my quarters first: there will be a whole party of us talking, singing, and making a noise, and we will all enter Worsted's quarters: there we shall find, no doubt, the man on the look-out, who will twig the whole of us, and take down our number. When we come back again we shall be in a state of excitement, of course, laughing, and rowing, and playing all sorts of pranks, and the Bumbailiff will have considerable difficulty in saying whether his man is among the lot or not. All he can do is to count the noses. If, therefore, we juniors carry out our parts pretty well, we can manage to retreat, bearing with us, not the body of Patroclus, but the body of Worsted. Now your quarters are admirably situated for his slipping in at your door; he may pass the night here, and walk to parade in the morning, while you can take possession of his couch for the night, and to-morrow go to parade. If you are stopped, you will after all be sure to be released upon giving an explanation who you are. Now then, is it agreed? if so, come along with me at once to Worsted's quarters."

"Well," said Montagu, "there can be no harm in that, so come along."

CHAPTER IX.

As Walduck and Montagu were walking, they saw a figure move in a suspicious manner beneath the shadow of one of the adjoining buildings.

Walduck gave Montagu a nudge on the arm, and said in an under voice:

"Look, at your left there. Do not you see a fellow skulking about wrapped up in a great big sort of a coachman's coat."

"Yes," said Ernest. "I see him. What is that he has got in his hand, it seems like a young fir tree?"

"Oh! no," said Walduck. "It is only one of the knotted sticks which those gentry always go about with. A sheriff's officer considers himself nothing if he does not carry timber enough in his hand to bear the colours of a regiment. Now, fancy that fellow—he will stand, watch, watch, watch, the whole of this night long, munching, I suppose, some miserable wretched biscuit, with his dirty jaws; and, even when morning breaks, that fellow will be still on duty, with his eyes as sharp as a lynx's, and so he will watch until the regiment starts, and, if in the meantime any opportunity arrives by an open door of slipping into Worsted's quarters, I suppose he will present him with that odious little bit of narrow paper so very disagreeable to one bearing her Majesty's commission."

"There you are quite out, Captain," roared out a vulgar voice at Walduck's elbow, which made him and Montagu start. "It is quite clear you have never been taken.

What we goes upon is a totally different process from that."

"Get out of my reach, you scoundrel, or I will annihilate you," said Walduck, angry with himself at having been made to start with the sudden apparition. "How dare you listen and try to overhear the private conversation of two gentlemen?"

Montagu turned suddenly round, and there stood a second sheriff's officer, very much the counterpart of the other, only stouter, thicker, and at the near gaze exhibiting those marked peculiarities which distinguish the children of Israel. His great coat was unbuttoned, and waistcoat crossed by a profusion of large gilt chain cable; his lips were bunchy and thick; his nose prominent and hooked; and, in his little sparkling black eyes, there lurked cunning enough to make or ruin half a world of debtors.

"He, he, he—that is more than you dare do, Captain," said the sheriff's officer, handling the enormous bludgeon in a very symptomatic manner—"It is all very well for you ossifers to swagger and so forth, but you daren't strike no civil officers, you know—you knows a trick worth two of that—you do."

"Get out of my way, sir," said Walduck. "If it were not for the infernal lawyers, by whom you beastly blackguards are backed up, the public indignation of England would grind you to powder."

"And don't you wish it would, though, and grind your creditors, too—eh, Captain?"

"Creditors, sir,—I have none," said Walduck, very indignantly.

"Has not you, though? Then you are just the gemman I want to come across. You must be in want of the 'ready,' I know, sir, to go to the Crimea. I have a friend would be very happy to do a little bill for you, dirt sheep, upon my honor, sir. If a gentleman has no creditors, I know he would do it for twenty per shent, or a very little mores, anyways."

"Get out of my way, you scoundrel: I

want none of your bills or your money, and a curse upon both of you."

"Well, at any rate, your honor, take a drop of brandy with us this cold night. I can sell you a dozen of this, very fine indeed—never saw the custom-house."

"Get out of my way, you rascal—I detest brandy and you too;" and Walduck dragged Montagu on; but the child of Moses was not to be thus put off.

Hanging in Walduck's rear, he said, "Ah! I likes your honour—you does abuse one with such warmth. I know you be a good friend, if I could only persuade you of it. Now do just try one of these cigars, sir: I can sell you a hundred of them. It is almost giving them away—'pon my life it is, s'help me Abram."

"Get out of my way, you infernal thief," said Walduck, turning round and making a dash towards him.

"Draw it mild, sir—draw it mild, sir," said the other sheriff's officer in the shade.

"He arn't got no cigars nor brandy neither; he is only trying to chaff and draw you out, and if you does strike him you will get into a mess."

"Yes, yes," said Montagu, pulling Walduck violently away, and entering Worsted's quarters, as they closed the door of which, they heard the two children of Israel raise a loud laugh at their expense.

"Who are those fellows laughing at?" asked Worsted when they had got in.

"Oh! that is the laugh of the besiegers," said Ernest.

"The infernal set of thieves!" said Walduck. "My dear fellow, independently of the obligation one feels to a brother officer, it would really do one's heart good to raise the siege of such a couple of ruffians as those outside. What are your plans for the night?"

"Well," said Worsted, "I hardly know whether I shall be able to succeed; but this is clear, that it would be the most provoking thing in the world to be taken by those infernal fellows just as the regiment is going on service."

"Oh! yes, indeed, indeed it would," said Montagu; "it would be the ruin of all your prospects in the army, unless you could get released in time to join the regiment before sailing."

"Of that I have no chance I can tell you; for if this infernal fellow, Doem, once gets hold of me for three hundred, I might just as well try to raise the monument, as on short notice to raise that sum. I will tell you therefore, what I purpose to do. Just about two o'clock in the morning, when those blackguards outside there are getting a little sleepy, and might suppose that I should be thinking of escape, I am going to make my servant dress up evidently in disguise, get out of my bed-room window upon the roof, throw down something to attract the attention of those rascals below (a piece of broken tile, or something of that sort); then, when once he sees that they are awake and watching him, he is to steal very cautiously along until he comes near the end of the gable: there he is to fasten a rope round the chimney, let himself quickly down, and bolt for an escape right out of the barracks. He is a capital runner, and, once outside the barrack-gates, he will very soon contrive to earth himself. These two fellows will away after him, never suspecting the trick: then I shall quietly leave my quarters and go over to yours, so that when the parade is formed I can slip out and join it without these fellows being present."

"Well, that is a very good run in its way—but suppose these fellows catch your servant, they will find out he is not the right man."

"No, but if they catch my servant outside the barrack-gates, you may depend they will catch a Tartar—they have no right to touch him, you know, and he will break a few of their bones in pure self-defence.

"Well," said Walduck, "I think it may answer."

"At any rate it will be capital fun," said Montagu; "and it will help to pass away the night, even if it it does not succeed. In the meantime, we will have a quiet hand at whist, and a bottle of claret, and drink a speedy surrender of Sebastopol."

The table was soon formed, the party sat down, supper made its appearance, and two o'clock gradually arrived.

The great event of the evening now was to come off.

Worsted called his servant in, and having inspected his disguise and pronounced it complete, furnished him with a rope; and while he went up to the window to make his escape, the candles were put out in the sitting-room below, in order that all hands might watch the effect upon the officers.

Presently they heard a tap — something

slid down from the roof and fell upon the ground.

"Ha!" they heard one of the officers say, "What is it?" Some whisper then passed between them, and they stole over the road on tiptoes, keeping their eyes fixed on the suspected roof. In order to do this, one of them stumbled backwards, fell down, and before the other could check himself he was over upon him.

The servant seized the favorable opportunity, whipped his noose round the chimney, slipped down the rope; and, before the officers were on their feet, away he was off like a deer.

"Help me, Abram, he's off!" said one of the officers to the other, adding an infinite number of oaths.

First, away bolted one, and then off ran the other after him.

As soon as they were fairly out of sight,

great were the rejoicings raised in the barrack-room.

"Hurrah! Hurrah! Well done. Nothing could have been better. Montagu, my boy, just go out, and see that the coast is clear, before I start."

"I will," said Ernest; and, stepping out, he looked carefully about him. Nothing was to be seen; but, hearing retreating footsteps, he followed their direction, and just caught a glimpse of the two sheriff's officers tearing along the high road, and in front of them the nimble-footed soldier, leaving them rapidly in the rear.

Hurrying back to quarters, he exclaimed, "Now, Worsted, my boy, now is your time: the enemy are in full retreat."

"Hurrah!" said Worsted, who, putting on his uniform as quickly as possible, crossed over to Montagu's quarters; and it was then agreed that Worsted should slip into the room of Montagu, who should give up his bed to Worsted.

Full of fun and merriment at the success of their stratagem, it was nearly three o'clock before all parties got to sleep, and dismal indeed was the call that awoke them just as day was breaking.

However, military time and military duty stand no putting off.

Ernest jumped to his feet, hastily completed his toilet, and, when it wanted only about two minutes of the parade hour, he looked through the window; and there, to his astonishment, stood the identical sheriff's officers. In an instant he popped back, but not in time to escape their sharp eyes.

"Hurrah! Hurrah! there he is. We knowed it was only a dodge. 'Twon't do, Cappen: you must come out of your shell in a few minutes," they cried, coming before his window, and exhibiting the most evident delight at being, as they thought, once more secure of their prey.

"Now, what is to be done," thought Ernest. "I do not want even to be taken in error by these men. Here, Miles," turning to his own servant, who had come to call and dress him, "Do you see any suspicious fellows lurking outside there?"

"Yes, your honor," said Miles.

"Ah! it is very shocking," said Ernest. "You would not think it, would you?"

"What, your honour?"

"That those are two spies of the Emperor of Russia?"

"Spies, your honor!" said Miles, opening his eyes in great astonishment—"I thought as how them were Captain Worsted's sheriff's officers."

"Dear me, Miles—to think how an intelligent soldier like you might be mistaken.—But they are very much in the way, Miles."

"Yes, your honor."

"I should think, that if some of those intelligent bystanders, who have come out to see the regiment turn out at day-break, could only know that these were Russian spies, I say I should not be surprised if they did not call out Russian spies!"

"I should not be surprised," said Miles, with a broad grin, "and very proper such Roossians should be known. I dare say, your honor, it would save their lives if they took a timely hint and got out of the way."

"Ha! ha! yes, Miles: it would be doing them a great service. It is a shocking thing, you know, to be taken for a Russian spy."

"A nod is as good as a wink, your honor, to a blind horse;" and away bolted Miles.

Going out of the quarters, he went up to the two sheriff's officers: "I say, young men, you had better take care of yourselves—you will be in a deuce of a scrape presently."

"What is the matter, my good soldier?"

"Oh! you need not come gammoning me, you know. There is a report got abroad in the regiment, that you are a couple of Roossian spies; and, if the populace only comes to understand how you Roossian spies have come here to write to the Emperor of Roossia all about our regiment, I would not stand in your shoes for a trifle."

"Russian spies," said both officers in a breath, "we are not, sir—we are not, sir."

"Oh! don't gammon me," said Miles. "They tell me that the Emperor of Roossia has got his spies everywhere. Spies! Spies! Russian spies!" said Miles, lifting his voice. "Get away from me. I abominate Roossian spies."

Every time the word was uttered, the horror of the poor unfortunate sheriff's officers seemed to increase; and well it might, for all the friends of the soldiers in the neighbourhood were now pouring into the barrack-yard to see the regiment parade.

"Spies! Russian spies!" said one to another. "We will soon spy them!"

"Here, my boy, which did you say were Russian spies?" said two or three of the stoutest of those bystanders.

But the sons of Israel did not wait for the answer. They very soon declared what was their sense of the subject; and, reading a horse-pond at least, if not a sound thrashing, in the glistening eyes of the enquirers, whose numbers every moment increased, they fairly took once more to their heels, and bolted off through the barrack-gate: the roar increasing still as they ran—"Russian spies! Russian spies!" until the two unfortunate Jews were out of sight from the barrack-yard, and the voices of the pursuers began to lessen in the distance.

As soon as Montagu saw the coast clear, he opened the door of his quarters, and walked out to join parade. In a few seconds after, the clock had struck.

CHAPTER X.

In military life, the dangers that threaten each individual are so numerous, the ordinary vexations of humanity dwindle to nothing in their presence.

When a man is perpetually contemplating the chances of being ordered out on a minute's notice, to face a duty where the chances are ten to one that he may be brought back to his quarters with a mortal wound, or left an unhonored corpse upon the battle-field, it is utterly impossible to produce much effect upon him by the minor miseries that torment the wealthy and the prosperous.

Before the regiment got to sea, they had a great many of these minor miseries to endure. In fact, moving from comfortable quarters, and being put on board a ship, is a horror in its way. Every man lost everything. Nothing was at hand. All things were uncomfortable, and there was no prospect of anything being better, until the ship arrived at her destination; for although, when she put out to sea, things settled down in their place a little, yet then came sea-sickness, and, to a landsman, the question is, whether, for the time, it is not almost equal to death itself. Then the misery and confusion of sea-sickness among a number of officers and troops, clogged with all their baggage on board a transport,—everything is out of its place—everything is strange—everything seems reeking with dirt, disorder, confusion, danger, and disaster—or at least they appear to be so to men accustomed to terrâ firma, and not easily able to conform to the succession of hardships that mark an existence at sea.

Still, amidst all these horrors and troubles, as fast as a man recovered from the distressing inertia of the voyage, the indomitable, and almost reckless good humour of the mind seized any little trifle on which to make itself happy,—cigars, claret, brandy-and-water, with liberal interpolations of whist, cheered away the few passing days that intervened between England and the Crimea.

The Nonsuch was a very fortunate regiment, as it was termed, for it went out in a magnificent ship, and certainly, as far as size went, she was magnificent; but the most magnificent ship in the world would not be able to obviate the inconveniences we have described.

Full of delight and joy were the troops when they found themselves passing through the romantic and rocky entrance of Balaclava.

Alas! they little knew that it was then, and not till then, that all their sorrows, horrors, troubles and disasters were to commence.

The place, which bore the appearance of a chasm rent in a mountain, letting in a deep tongue of the sea, was crowded with shipping.

With considerable difficulty a spot was found, in which the troops could land.

With the natural inclination of soldiers to shew themselves smart and tidy to the army on their first arrival, the men went on shore in the best order their sea-voyage would permit; but if they thought the decks of the transport uncomfortable and ill-arranged, great, indeed, was their horror at contemplating the wharf and roads of Balaclava in a state of complete mire.

Before they had gone half a mile towards the camp, all of the men, and most of the officers, were picking their way almost over their boot-tops in mud, and some of them in endeavouring to extricate their feet from this quagmire, lost their boots.

It is impossible to imagine the disgust and foreboding of ill that prevailed throughout the regiment, when they found that, in the first step towards the field of fame, the most common foresight in the world had not been used, to provide an ordinary road between the besiegers' trenches and the spot where all the materials of the siege were to be landed, including the men and provisions.

And those trenches, what were they but a bitter mockery and mere death-traps? unless they could be fairly supplied with the materials of war, men, and provision first, before all the rest.

Before the troops had got half way to Sebastopol, it came on to rain—the cold, mizzling, drizzling rain, which set in as if it had quite made up its mind to last the whole of the evening, and perhaps the following day.

On arriving at the camp, they found that no orders had been issued for their provisions or their tents; and there they were halted wet through, miry up to their knees, hungry, dispirited, not knowing where to lay their heads or to procure wherewithal to quench their appetities, marvelling what kind of commanders those could be, who thus received reinforcements; and full of the most deadly forebodings as to what would be the issue of a warfare pursued under such a system.

"What is the meaning of this? What can it mean?" said Spinney to one or two of the officers who gathered round him. "Has any accident happened? Is the commander-in-chief dead? What is the meaning of it? I never read or heard of any army with a secure base of operation upon the sea, commanded by a vigorous fleet, with a boundless supply for the commissariat, and every other necessary that could be required from a wealthy country at home—I never heard, in all that I have ever read of military proceedings, of an army in such circumstances, only six miles from the coast, being in this deplorable plight and disorder! What is the meaning of it, Major Fussey?"

"Egad, I do not know," said Fussey, shrugging his shoulders. "I spoke to Colonel Lossefysh several times on our way out here, but I could get nothing out of him except muttered oaths innumerable; but who he was blessing he did not communicate to me."

"Well, I think, Fussey, he was very prudent in that."

"Oh! precisely so, precisely. It reminds me very much of the state of things after Walcheren, just when the army came home to Deal. The Prince Regent came to call upon my father (the Prince Regent, you know, was wrapped up in my father), and the Duke of York was with him. My father said, 'What is the news, your Royal Highness, from the

Walcheren expedition?' 'I tell you what, Fussey,' said his Royal Highness to my father, 'I can give you every possible information about the Walcheren expedition. I have just been talking it over to York, who has now come back from Holland, and I see exactly how the Walcheren expedition stands. The Walcheren expedition is nothing more nor less than a case of fever. The whole army may be divided into three classes—every officer and man in it, is either dying of the Walcheren fever, recovering from the Walcheren fever, (and they are very few), or else he is dead of the fever, and the last are in the majority, and so the less that is said about them the better.' The Prince of Wales, you know, was wrapped up in my father."

"Egad, I wish we could convey to the Prince of Wales of our day, and those who are about him, the smallest notion of what is the state of things in which we are wrapped up out here," said Worsted. "It is more discouraging, disgusting, and disgraceful than it is possible to conceive."

"Is Ensign Montagu there?" said Colonel Loosefysh, riding up at this moment.

"Yes, sir," said Ernest.

"Be so good as to take my horse, which the orderly is leading, and ride over with this note, will you, to Lord George Superfine, of the Commander-in-Chief's staff. Lord George and I were very intimate once upon a time, and I have just told him we are out here, and there seems to be nobody who knows anything of us, or how to give us any thing—that we have no food, no tents; and, as I came along the camp to-day, it seemed to me to be a case of 'no nothing at all that ought to be here.' Just let those chaps on the staff know what a state of ruin and confusion everything seems to be in around us; and you can tell him (though I have not put it in my note), that the folks at home are beginning to say, that it is the fine young gentlemen of the staff who ought to be a little more active; but do it in a quiet way you know: and I send you, Mr. Montagu," he added in a low voice, "to do this, because if your remonstrance is not liked, it would be less thought of from a man who knows less of the rules of the service than an old stager."

"Very well, sir," said Ernest, and mounting the horse held by the Colonel's orderly, he turned his head, and galloped to a low but neat looking two-storied house, in which the Commander-in-Chief had his quarters.

As he drew near to the Commander-in-Chief's dwelling, he saw two young gentlemen with moustaches, very nicely and very comfortably dressed, all things considered: they wore much about the same sort of dress that is seen in most English gentlemen's country houses on the first of September, when the day has arrived for the doom of the partridges—in short they had on their shooting coats and tweed trowsers, with the everlasting cigar in the mouth of each.

"What the deuce can these fellows be?" thought Montagu. "They are taking it very easily, considering only a day or two ago the terrific battle of Inkerman happened. What can they be? They cannot be officers of the army surely, and what do civilians do here with shooting coats on? Well, if it is only for the curiosity of speaking to them I will do it." Then turning his horse towards these two young gentlemen, who seemed blessed with so much leisure, he did not address them in the words of Virgil: "Quis Deus hæc otia fecit," though he might have done so; or translated it into the vernacular by saying, "who the devil gave you leave to take it so coolly?"

"Gentlemen, may I ask you to tell me where I am to find Lord George Superfine?"

"A-ah, you are ve-wy lucky," said one of the two moustached gentlemen, pausing in their lounging walk with the least possible elevation of the eyebrows.

"My name is Superfine," said the other moustache.

"O! indeed," said Ernest, "I am exceedingly fortunate. I bring you a note, Lord George, from Colonel Loosefysh, who commands our regiment, the Nonsuch, just landed."

"A-a-ah!" said Superfine, with a good deal of fashionable drawl still left in him, notwithstanding all the Russian balls he had recently attended since he left those of Almack's. "I hope Loosefysh is well. Tell him—a—I have not forgotten what a good hand he used to hold at écarté."

"I will," said Montagu; "but here is a note he sent you by me, and he will be much obliged to you if you can help us in a quiet way."

"Help you!" said Lord George, elevating his eyebrows: "dear me—a—" and here the drawl seemed to get very strong again. "A—you—surely cannot be—a—wanting—a—any help already—a—can you?"

"'Pon my life—a—'pon honor," said the other man, "a—it really is most disgusting to be on the staff of this army. It appears to me that—a—every body wants——every other body to help them in—a—every possible way."

"Ah! I see your duties on the staff are very fatiguing," said Montagu.

"Oh!" said the other man, who was the Honorable Mr. Tapeling, "the duties of this staff are really quite—a—disgusting. One would think, by the constant application to one, that it was only necessary to be made a staff-officer to have the labours of Hercules forced upon one's shoulders, and the Augean stables to cleanse out every morning. A—I do not understand it; a—I do not understand it at all."

"O! I pity you," said Montagu; "but you know the remedy is very short. Appointments on the staff are always prized however erroneously. You can always resign."

When Montagu said this, the Honourable Mr. Tapeling looked at him with a sort of mute and ineffable contempt from the point of his shako down to his horse's hoofs; and then, as if he were utterly unable to express the hundredth part of the contempt he felt, turned round upon his heel, took out his cigar-case, and lit a fresh weed. "Superfine, I am going on to the a—stables, to see Handicap fed. When you have attended to that little affair of a—business, you will find me there."

"Aw, very good, Tapeling." Then, added Lord George, turning to Montagu, "Give my kind regards to Colonel Loosefysh: tell him I am very glad to have heard from him. I am just going down to my stables, to look at my horse for a few minutes. If you will come down, I will shew you as fine a bit of horseflesh as you would wish to see; and then I will come back with you to head-quarters, and one of my orderlies shall make some enquiries about the tents and all those sort of things. Will you take a cigar?" drawing his case out of his pocket.

"Thank you," said Ernest. "We have had a very disagreeable day to day: we are all wet through, and miserable, and wretched, to say nothing of that nameless oppression that a man feels when he first comes on shore out of a ship, which has been his home for some weeks."

"Oh! yes, a—I understand all that sort of thing, as I wrote home to my mother the other day. 'The army has to rough it a little, but it will soon shake down into a state of efficiency; and then, when all these feather bed grumblers, you know, are sent back sick to the rear, the fighting boys will do all the business that is requisite.'"

"Have you many sick?" said Ernest.

"Oh! a—why! aw—well. Ah—I don't know much of the medical staff; we don't associate much, you know, with doctors, and that kind of people, you know. It is not the thing; they are always making some fuss or bother about something. Egad, I believe, that if the Commander-in-Chief bundled all the doctors into a boat, and sent them all home together, we should be just as well without them as we are with them, a pack of grumbling civilians. A—quite a mistake in the service, I think, giving them uniform, or recognising them in any way as an efficient part of the army. Well, now, here are our stables, you see; we have knocked up these very speedily have we not? Here, orderly, take this horse, while you just get down, Mr. —a—a, you did not give me your name, and Colonel Loosefysh has omitted it in his note."

"My name is Montagu."

"Oh! Mr. Montagu, I beg your pardon. Well, now, look here, you see; considering we have got these stables up in a hurry, now they are very nicely done, are they not? Here you see, is this horse's manger, a sort of little loose-box for him, you know; then, as the cold weather comes on, we shall nail outside the stables some felt, or some tarred canvass, or something of that sort. This is my favourite charger; he is looking in splendid condition, is he not, the old rascal? He has not had much to do since Inkerman, but he does not forget the grub for all that, four feeds a day, besides hay."

"Oh! you have some hay, have you?" said Montagu.

"Oh, of course, plenty of hay. What made you ask such a question?"

"There was some report in England about the fodder being scarce."

"It never reached my ears," said Superfine. "The hay was packed and compressed, and sent out. Of course the horses of the staff, you know, cannot do without hay. Of course the staff horses must be looked to,—a most important thing. What is the use of an army without horses to its staff?"

"Dear me," said Montagu, "you have a

number of horses here. How many have you, Lord George?"

"Well, two of mine died at Varna. I have only three here now, but they are looking in very good condition, arn't they?" And Lord George began patting this horse, and that horse, and the other horse, while the honourable Mr. Tapeling went and gave his horse an additional handful of corn, just to encourage him in knowing his master.

"Have you any news of that brute, the Czar?" said Lord George, sitting himself on an empty cask, and kicking it idly with his heel, while he went on with his cigar.

"No, not much news of him, but the chief fear in England is that he will gather the whole of his forces, and pour down into the Crimea in such masses, that our unfortunate army, valiant as it is, will almost be eaten up by numbers. The friends of Russia say, that the Czar is able to command any amount of men, and cares no more about losing 20, or 30,000 in a battle or two, than he cares about having his nails cut when they are grown too long."

"Ah! yes—yes—yes—a—that is awkward, certainly. He has a great command of men. I was in hopes that you could have told us that rumours of peace were progressing."

"But," said Montagu, "our fellows would be infinitely disgusted if there were any talk of peace. We come out here envying you boys who have had such chances of distinguishing yourselves and getting promotion. We look to have a few more Alma's, and Inkerman's, and that sort of thing, and to make up for the charge at Balaclava."

"Ah! well, I should not object to the Inkermans or the Almas. As long as there is fighting to be done we flatter ourselves on the Staff that we all feel pretty much at home at that, but what I dislike so much is the beastly wet weather—all this mud, and the constant grumble, grumble, grumble, that goes on from these beetle-crushers from morning to night, but I beg your pardon; I forgot that you were not in the Cavalry."

"Well, but if you dislike the grumbling that goes on here in the Camp, what would you only feel if you heard what was said in England?"

"Ah, indeed, and do they say anything in England?"

"Rather," said Ernest.

"Dear me, and what do they say in England? I am sure they ought to be infinitely indebted to us, wasting our existence in all this wretchedness, and dirt, and misery."

"I do not see much of it in your stable," said Ernest, looking round. "You seem pretty comfortable here, and I suppose the house at head quarters is not much less comfortable than the servant's stables."

"Ah—a—yes—you know, for the matter of that—a—if any man's comfort is valuable in the army it is the comfort of the Commander-in-Chief and his staff—every man must admit that—but the place is such a wretched place, there is not a single pheasant to be had; if there were a few woods now, and one could find a cock or two occasionally, or could ride to hounds now and then, when the work is not very pressing."

"Well, but," said Montagu, "I think the work is very pressing; for all this time our unfortunate fellows are wet through, covered with mud, as hungry as wolves, nothing to eat—nobody seems to be able to tell them where their tents have got to, or where they are to pitch them when they come."

"Ah! they must grumble a little at first, you know, they will soon find that sort of fun evaporates. Just wait till I have finished my cigar, and I will go up to the house with you and see what is to be done."

"Yes, but by the time your cigar is finished there will be a half-an-hour's more daylight gone. Come, come at once, and smoke it in your way up to the house."

"'Pon my life, Tapeling, did you ever hear anything like the exigency of these beetle-crushers—everything must be done for them —they cannot help themselves to anything—they want everything done at once, and no time to do it in—however, poor fellows, I suppose we must oblige them—so come, we will go up and see whether there is anything in this after all," and tearing up Loosefysh's note in small pieces, very deliberately, he threw them on the ground, and turning out of the stables they all three walked towards the house at head quarters.

CHAPTER XI.

The head quarters were at a long, low building with five windows in front, and two stories high; the front appeared to be well whitewashed, and formed a complete contrast even in the hazy weather and declining day, with the wretchedness and dirt with which Montagu had been struggling ever since he landed.

In one of the rooms of the house was seen through the windows the fitful blaze of a good fire, which spoke out with a degree of warmth and homeliness, which, simple as such a circumstance might appear at home, awoke powerful feelings in the melancholy breast of the young Ensign.

Just as they approached the door, some other officer came up to Lord George Superfine, and after a word or two exchanged in a low tone, Superfine said:

"You just wait there a moment or two and I will come out to you,"—then turning to Ernest, he said, "You follow me, if you please."

Lord George walked into the house, and showed our hero into a room where one or two other officers were seated waiting, but where there was no fire.

"Just take a chair here until I can ascertain the facts you want to know, and I will return to you."

Five minutes passed away—a quarter of an hour—half an hour, slowly and sadly expanded into three quarters of an hour, still poor Montagu continued kicking his heels, looking at everyone who went in and out, to see if he could recognise Lord George—there remained his poor famished horse walking up and down in the hands of the orderly, and he himself almost ready to faint with hunger, fatigue, and weariness.

At last when an hour had nearly been completed, Montagu began to deliberate whether it was not possible that Lord George had found some other opportunity of commencing a fresh cigar, and also whether it was not desirable that he should ride back to his Colonel, even though he took no answer. At this moment the door opened and in stepped Lord George.

" Two or three officers rose to speak to him, and each man began his application with, " I have been waiting here for the last hour," but singling out Montagu he simply said to the others, " I will attend to you presently," and then went out of the room, and put a three cornered note into Ernest's hand.

"Give that to Colonel Loosefysh with my kind regards, will you, and say, I hope to be riding over his way to-morrow. I am sorry I am so busy with all these various bothers—I must wish you good bye now," and beckoning to the orderly, who had brought up Montagu's horse, Lord George turned round on his heel, and went back into the little room to speak to some other officers awaiting there.

Well, thought Ernest, I do not know much of the art of war, but this seems to me a strange mode of conducting it. One thing was evident, that it was Montagu's duty to gallop forward as fast as he could to Colonel Loosefysh with the reply he bore.

As he came up to the Regiment, he found it pretty much in the same state as when he left it.

"Here, Montagu, what a deuce of a time you have been gone," said Fussey, rather sulkily, as Ernest cantered up to him.

"Where is Colonel Loosefysh?" said our hero, pulling up.

"Oh! he will be back here in a minute. He has merely ridden towards the trenches. What is the reply to the Colonel's note?"

"I am sure I cannot say," said Ernest—"here it is"—pulling out Lord George's note from his breast coat pocket—"I only hope it contains something more satisfactory than my reception at head quarters was; I was kept waiting for an hour, in a room without a fire, and had not even a piece of dry bread, or a glass of water offered to me."

"This seems to be altogether a very odd mode of conducting war," said Fussey.

"I do not understand it," said Spinney.

"Oh! I understand it perfectly," said Walduck.

"Well then, pray explain it to me, will you," said Fussey. "What does it mean?"

"It simply means that the army is going to the dogs as fast as it can rattle, and that those who ought to take care of us know nothing of the way to do so."

The other officers shrugged their shoulders at this speech.

At this moment up came Colonel Loosefysh.

"Here is an answer, sir, I have just brought back to your note, Colonel Loosefysh."

"Why, what in the name of all the powers has kept you so long Mr. Montagu?"

"I have been kept waiting an hour at head quarters."

"An hour at head quarters—do you mean to say that Lord George kept you waiting an hour at head quarters?"

"Yes, Colonel Loosefysh, and more."

"Why, what the deuce was he about?"

"Oh! he was very busy."

"Busy," said Loosefysh, taking the note. "What was he so busy about that he could not write me a note like this?"

"Smoking a cigar," said Montagu, "that seemed to be his chief business."

"I should think so," said Loosefysh.

"Why there is nothing in this note except a line in pencil.

"DEAR LOOSEFYSH,

"I have not been able to find out the information you require.

"Ever yours, in haste,

"GEORGE SUPERFINE."

"Why, this is enough to drive a man mad —Major Fussey let the men stack their arms, and see if they can grub up a few roots to make a fire—I must ride over myself, to headquarters, and see if I can find in what division we are to be brigaded."

"What are the men to eat, Colonel Loosefysh?" said the Major.

"Eat," repeated Loosefysh, "Just exactly what you and I have had to eat—anything they can get," and with a hearty shower of curses, Loosefysh clapped spurs to his horse, and away he went.

CHAPTER XII.

The evening was beginning rapidly to advance, darkness had set in; still the rain fell with a cold miserable wind from the northwest, which seemed to chill one to the very marrow, when Colonel Loosefysh returned, and the officers instantly gathered round him.

"By this and by that, Fussey," said the Colonel—"If this is a taste of the way we are to go on in this war, the sooner we take Sebastopol the better. It seems it was all a blunder ordering us to march to the camp to-day: it was not intended that we should have come out here until to-morrow, and therefore we wern't to have orders to move till the day after."

"Why, how could that be, Colonel? Is not that a little bit of a bull?"

"Ah! you know what I mean: you know our orders wern't intended to reach us till to-morrow, and then we were to march out to-morrow afternoon—that is as far as I can make out; for it would puzzle old Harry to understand what some of these fellows are meaning."

"But how about our rations, Colonel Loosefysh?" said Spinney.

"That is the very thing that is in fault. It seems our rations are all at Balaclava, and we are not to draw rations on shore to-day. We were to have had our rations on board the ship to-day, and we have only rations on shore from to-morrow; so that, if we had done what was right, we should have brought up our rations to-night and gone without food to-day."

"That statement does not seem very clear," said Fussey.

"Clear," said Loosefysh: "Och! the only thing that is clear in the matter to me is, that there is nothing clear in any business connected with this affair out here, whatever it may be at home. To think of a whole regiment being ordered where they wern't wanted, and leaving behind them those rations which were wanted, and those rations not even ordered on the proper day!"

"Well, but whose fault is it?"

"Whose fault is it? I can tell you what, Major Fussey: you will be a cleverer man than your humble servant, if you could find out whose fault it is; for that is the very thing I have been trying to find out ever since I left here, and I am just as wise as when I started."

"Well, but what are the men to do for

food? Are they to go without food all night?"

"Well, not quite so bad as that: as a particular favor, we are to receive a half ration presently from some of the commissariat people; and the men will get half a gill of rum a-piece, which will help them to go through the night."

"And how about the tents?"

"Ah! by Jove, there is the tent, Major Fussey, and we will have to sleep under it," said Loosefysh, pointing up with his finger to the sky, where there was a tent indeed of dark thick lowering scud, pouring continuous drizzle, drizzle, on the unfortunate aspirants to fame.

At this moment, the voice of an officer was heard, enquiring, "Where is Colonel Loosefysh?"

"Here I am," said Loosefysh. "Do you want me? I suppose you have come with the half rations for the Nonsuch regiment."

"I have come to the Nonsuch regiment," said the Officer, "but not with the half rations. I do not belong to the commissariat department, but I bring an order for a contingent to the trenches to-night of fifty men and two subalterns."

"The trenches to-night!" said Loosefysh in surprise, taking the order in his hand. "Are you come to order men to the trenches that have not been able to get bit or sup since they landed from the ship to-day? They are dead beat with quagging through the bog, and not a dry rag on them or a tent to cover them. Is it the trenches that you are come to ask for?"

"That is my order, Colonel Loosefysh."

"By this and by that, sir, if you had come to order us to go through fire and water and stone walls, and walk into Sebastopol, I would say, come and welcome; but if I order my men in the trenches to-night, in the state they are now, how the deuce do you think I shall ever get them out again?"

"Really, Colonel Loosefysh, I do not know. I am not aware of the exact condition of your regiment. I did not even know it was landed to-day, much less that it had not been rationed: perhaps I had better go back to the Adjutant General, and inform him of the position in which you are placed."

"No, sir, no, sir. An order to go on duty is an order to go on duty. I will obey it, but if the men die off like rotten sheep, it is only just what we have a right to expect: therefore, tell the Adjutant General the state in which my regiment is, that I have made you acquainted with these facts, and that I hasten to obey your order. Here, Mr. Montagu, you have seen a fire to-night at any rate. I dare say you had a smell of the Commander-in-chief's dinner, which was roasting: that was more than any other officer had. You and Mr. Walduck take fifty men of your company, and go into the trenches to-night."

"Very good, sir," said Montagu.

"Stay, sir," said the officer who brought the order: "if you will be good enough to let your men wait half-an-hour, I will come back and inform you what the Adjutant General says under the circumstances you have mentioned." The officer turned round without waiting for an answer, and away he went.

"I tell you what, Fussey," said Loosefysh, turning round and speaking in an under tone of voice, but the other officers still heard him; "they were lucky fellows, those brave boys that died at Inkerman and Balaclava. By this and by that if this is the way we are to waste our lives from sheer stupidity, and folly, and general ignorance, may I be hanged drawn, and quartered; if I would not rather be shot by a file of my own men!"

At this moment in the dark gloom of the evening, a couple of mules were seen approaching, under the command of some of the authorities of the commissariat, and this turned out to be the long-desired half rations.

It was speedily delivered out to the poor famishing men, who received it most thankfully. The great majority of them ate their salt pork, raw, gradually chewed their biscuit, and swallowed down the wine-glass full of rum with a little water; but when it came to the officers' turn to take such food, after a long day's toil, all of them declined the meat, a few of them drank the spirit: there was coffee to be sure, but it was green or unroasted, and about as useless as pebbles on the sea-beach—a small supply of biscuit, therefore, and a little water, formed their only food.

About an hour after this time, as no notice reached Colonel Loosefysh that his men were not wanted in the trenches, he conceived it his duty to supply the intimated contingent. Fifty men were told off, and placed under the command of Walduck, and Montagu accompanying him, they marched down to the front.

To a novice, in the art of war, like Montagu, there was something amusing as well as tremendously grand and awful, in the perpetual din and roar of heavy cannon battering Sebastopol; and although it was feebly replied to by the fire of the besieged, still every now and then one of the enemies' bombs hurled its shell through the air, making a bright arch of fire, succeeded by a deadly explosion wherever the shell happened to alight.

As they drew nearer the trenches, the frequency and neighbourhood of these disagreeable gentry increased, and when at last Ernest saw Walduck jump into what appeared to be a hideous ditch, nearly up to the knees in water, and he himself was compelled to follow, he began to realise for the first time all the glories of war.

"Egad, Walduck," said our hero, "is this the sort of place that we are to pass the night in?"

"Yes," said Walduck, "we may have the good luck to be able to remain here if we are not shot, and buried before the morning."

"Upon my life, there is something terrific in the effect of this cold work on the feet."

"Oh! never mind your feet," said Walduck, "Take care you do not pop your head above the trenches or you may have a bullet through your noddle before you know where you are. That is it—so stoop down, my men, stoop down, do not expose your heads—come along;" and away they went, paddling along like so many geese with many a wild and strangely sounding joke, even in the midst of all the dirt, misery, blood, and danger which surrounded them.

At last they arrived at the point where their services were required, and then, while some remained ready to defend the trenches, in case of a surprise, others proceeded to work with pick and shovel to execute fresh works, or to repair those that were injured.

"Do they always go on firing at this terrific rate?" said Montagu, to another of the officers, who appeared to be more seasoned to this kind of labour.

"Oh, no," said the other, "there is a little more row to night, you know, because we expect a sortie presently—these fellows always commence with very heavy fire, and, after they have made an effort as if they were going to pound the earth to pieces, we shall have presently two or three thousand Russians, more or less, rushing out to see if they cannot take our works in flank, and then comes the fun in repelling them."

"Ah! yes—Ah! very funny—very indeed," and at this moment it must be confessed, that in the mind of poor Ernest, there rose up sundry charming but distant images, the foremost of which were home, a snug room, and comfortable library—a quiet fire—a nice book—a warm cup of tea, and the image of a fair heroine marvellously like Miss Wyndham, together with a strong recollection of all the arguments which she had used to cure him of his scarlet fever, and induce him to take up a black coat instead of a red one. "Poor girl," thought Ernest, "if she could conceive one-tenth of the horrors that surround us at this moment how truly would she deem all her warnings have come to pass. What in the name of fortune brings me here? Can it be possible that I have been supreme ass enough to come to this spot, because the Czar of Russia, the Sultan of Turkey, and Lord John Russell have not been able to agree upon a point of public policy? Well, there are fools in the world to be sure, but of all the fools in the world, I appear to be the greatest."

At this moment a cry was heard, "Here come the Russians!"

"Now, my boys, fix bayonets," cried Walduck, but the words were scarcely out of his mouth, and Montagu's eyes were still fixed upon him, when he suddenly threw up his sword arm with a convulsive start; a deep groan followed, as he staggered for a space or two, and then fell backwards. Two or three men rushed to him in a minute, and began to carry him to the rear.

Montagu saw what followed, and with admirable coolness, remembering that his men were all fresh under fire, made no vain attempt to follow Walduck, but turning towards his own soldiers —

"Steady, my lads, steady," cried he, forgetting all his philosophic musings in the excitement of the moment, "Do not throw a shot away, my boys, until you can see the whites of their eyes plainly." At least, thought he, that always was soldierly advice in the days of Crawford's fighting Brigade, and I do not see why it should not tell yet.

"We'll be steady enough, sir," cried the men, warming up at the approach of danger, and delighted to see that their young Ensign was ready for the work of commanding them.

The heavy firing of the batteries had ceased —a quick running tramp of innumerable feet was heard, and a line of light opened right and left, and the quick firing of musketry, and the hissing of innumerable balls were instantly heard around them.

"Hold your fire, my men, hold your fire—not yet, not yet," cried Ernest, looking anxiously through the smoke, to watch the approaching figures of the Russians; then as they came bristling up, scrambling and running forward, and gradually developed amidst the dim and intermittent light of exploding shells, and rattling musketry, he, at last, perceived their faces plainly.

"There, my boys, straight before you. Ready! Present! Fire!"

Sharp as the words, the men of the Nonsuch Regiment delivered the fire of the Minie Rifles, and, as the flash went forth, so down went the Russian line before them, as if some vast and unseen knife had mowed them like human grass where they fell.

"Well done, my boys," cried Montagu, all thoughts of home, and, of everything else but the "*certaminis gaudia*," being utterly forgotten. "Now, my hearties, mount your rampart, and give them the cold steel," and seizing a firelock from a soldier who had fallen near him, our hero clapped his shoulder to that of a private next to him, mounted the rampart with them, and charged down upon the Russian line attempting to re-form.

"Bravo—well done! Well done, gallant Nonsuch," cried an old veteran officer, coming up at this moment, and beholding this gallant feat—it was Major Harty of the ——th. "Go ahead, my boys—you shall be well supported," and following with his own men, in an extended line they drove the Russians in full retreat once more up to their own works as far as it was safe to go, bayonetting a large number, and capturing several prisoners.

As soon as this sortie was repulsed, Ernest found himself surrounded by a number of the men, shaking hands with him, and thanking him in all sorts of ways for his gallantry, while presently up came Major Harty, adding his commendations to all the other less scientific, but not less sincere plaudits of the men around him.

"Where is poor Walduck?" said Ernest, who now, for the first time, allowed to escape him, the knowledge that his senior officer was down.

"O! then, your honor, he is only comfortably wounded," said Corporal Pipeclay: "a bit of broken shell struck him on the breast, and just knocked the breath out of him. A bit of one of the splinters caught him on the funny bone and threw his arm up, but I do not think the arm is broken; and, bating that he is spitting a little blood or so, I hope there is not much the matter."

"Have we lost many men in this little business, Sergeant?" said Montagu, turning round to his next in command.

"O! your honor, there are a few of the

boys tumbled over of course, for the fire was sharp when it came upon us at first, but I do not think there are above half a dozen. And now the Nonsuch have drawn blood, won't they know where to go and suck the Russian again? Ah! it will do the regiment all the good in the world, your honor: it will put their spirits up, and stand them in the stead of a pint of rum. Troth, then, I wish that hard fighting was the worst of it we had here; we would soon settle the business."

"Shall we have any more sorties to-night, Major?" said Montagu, addressing Major Harty.

"Oh! I think not—I think not. They are generally content with one whacking a night; they are very moderate boys. What a pity it is we cannot give the Czar a turn, instead of his poor soldiers."

"Well, then," said our hero, "if you think they will keep quiet for the rest of the night, we may as well send our wounded men to the rear at once."

"I have given orders for it already. There is an Assistant Surgeon here, and you may tell off half a dozen of your men to carry the wounded to him directly."

Directing an orderly to shew the way, Montagu turned round to see to this duty, and the business of the pick, spade, and shovel went on once more as before; while the numerous batteries again resumed their deadly shower of hissing shot and blazing shell with still greater rapidity of fire.

CHAPTER XIII.

"Where is the Signal-Lieutenant?" said the Captain of the Commander in Chief's Flag Ship in the Black Sea, on the day following that described in the last chapter. "What Ship is that in the offing?"

"Here am I, sir," said the Signal-Lieutenant, answering immediately at the elbow of his superior. "I was just coming to report to you, sir, that it is Her Majesty's ship Saucebox from Constantinople and England."

"O! it is the Saucebox come to join, is it?

Very well, I will go and report to the Admiral. I am glad she has made her number at last. All sorts of letters and packages are coming out by her."

Away went the Flag Captain to convey to the Commander-in-Chief the fact, that Her Majesty's ship, Saucebox, had just thrown out the bunting which conveyed her name.

"Oh! Oh! Saucebox from England," said a little Middy; "I will go down and give her name in the gun-room. I know there are loads of things coming out by her. I am to get a new pea jacket, with flushing trowsers and waistcoat."

Down hurried the Middy into the gun-room of the flag-ship, to communicate this intelligence to one or two friends who had been advised by their parents that articles had been shipped on board this vessel.

"The Saucebox!" said Lord Albert Plantagenet. "Ah! I suppose that is one of your horrid vulgar hybrids, between a passengers' steamboat and one of the gallant old frigates of other days."

"Yes, my tulip, you may say that," said Curtis, a square-shouldered young reefer. "She is one of that class so much wanted in these days—things born of genius and industry, and relying upon her worth for preferment, and not upon the worn out traditions of the last war, which concealed more blunders and more inefficiency, than the pyramids ever buried kings; and which only did not come to light, because in those days there was no *Times* Own Correspondent."

"Upon my life, Curtis, I really wish you would get rid of these low ideas about the *Times* and the *Times* Correspondent; as if Her Majesty's service, or Her Majesty's government, or Her Majesty's Commander-in-Chief, would take the slightest notice of those pen and ink gentry, who have nothing to do but to go titling and tatling about from the camp to the fleet and from the fleet to the camp, making a fuss about trifles, when, but for them everything would go as smooth as a marriage bell."

"Ah! you allude to the marriage of the Right Honourable the Lady Caroline Fitz Trousseau with the Right Honourable Lord Augustus Disennui, whose father came over of course with William the Conqueror. All those kinds of marriages, and that sort of thing, may flow smoothly enough no doubt; and the only use for which they would permit the press to exist, if they could possibly so order it, would be to chronicle what dresses were worn by the half a dozen bridesmaids; and how the highly descended bridegroom was accompanied by this scion of Twaddle-dom and that descendant of puerility, and how the ceremony was performed by the Honourable and Reverend Mr. Suchatithe, assisted by the Reverend Lord George Easterdue and the Reverend Canon Law and the Honourable and Reverend this that and the other, brothers of the noble bridegroom. No doubt all this would be smooth enough, but there is one great thing which interrupts its smoothness, my dear fellow."

"Ah! indeed. What is that?" said Lord George, yawning.

"Why the public have so much of it, they are quite sick of it, and poor John Bull begins at last to perceive that lords and ladies are all very well in their way; but, when they are stupid people, they are nothing more nor less than so many titled bores, whom he, John Bull, has ennobled to much the same end, as Sinbad put the old man on his shoulders to ride him to death."

"Ah! it is all very fine for low people to talk in that way of one of the greatest institutions in Europe, the English aristocracy; but I should like to know where you would have been without a House of Lords by this time?"

"No doubt yours is a very proper question, Lord Plantagenet. Without the House of Lords, England would have lacked a great deal of good, and I hope she will never be without her House of Lords; but, my dear fellow, it is the toadyism, and the flatterers, and the tuft hunters, and the place hunters, and the sinecure holders, and the abuse defenders—these are the men who are labouring, though they do not intend it, to pull down the House of Lords. Depend upon it, the House of Lords will never fall in England, so firmly attached are the people of England to the House of Lords as an institution; the House of Lords, I say, will never fall until it falls by the weight of its own abuse; and, let me tell you, its abuses are hanging heavily enough upon it just at present. Those are the friends of the House of Lords who wish to lop off all odious selfish excrescences, and let it trust to its own merits; just as you and I would do, if we were commanding this magnificent line of battle ship, and found ourselves caught in such a gale of wind that it became a question whether we should cut our masts or go bang on a lee shore."

"Oh! of course in such a case I should cut the masts by the board and save the ship."

"Very well, then, my old codger, you just write home to your governor, the Marquis, will you, and tell him, if he wants to keep the House of Lords right with the people, let him persuade his brother peers to attend more frequently in their places in Parliament and show a keener interest in the rights of the people."

"Rights of the people? what do you mean? what rights of the people are invaded in these days?"

"The first and best of all rights, the right of being purely and properly represented in Parliament. At present, seats in the House of Commons are bought and sold for money almost as openly as potatoes in a market place. Any cheesemonger or prize-fighter may buy a seat in the House of Commons for four thousand pounds or less. Confidence in the House of Commons is rapidly lowering, the franchise is scandalously restricted, the taxes recklessly imposed, and the public resources lavishly wasted; corruption is creeping into general tolerance, and the end of these things must be danger to the commonwealth, in whose injury no men can suffer so deeply as the peerage, for they hold the largest and best stakes in the country."

"But how are the peers to avert these evils?"

"Simply by exercise of their wills and intellects. The House of Lords form a body of the most clever, experienced, and powerful men in the kingdom—let them but once embrace the task of reforming the House of Commons, and all England to a man would back the House of Lords in doing it."

"Aye, but the question is, in what way can they do it?"

"By the resistless way of calling public opinion to their aid. By exposing the present corrupt and debasing system in their debates and speeches, and by giving the country an opportunity of rallying to their support in public meetings—by introducing some gentle and progressive measure for extending the franchise to the well conducted and intellectual classes, and by making bribery felony—all the rest would speedily follow."

"Ah! I should like, now, to argue that question with you a little further."

"My dear fellow—it is too plain to admit of an argument, and I hear the paddles of the Saucebox heaving-to under our quarter, so I shall go up and see what box my jolly old dad has sent from Devonshire to me."

Curtis jumped up and was running away to the hatchway, when Lord Albert called after him.

"I say, Curtis, it's a mighty small box your

governor would send to you if your worthy conservative baronet knew the radical opinions you had imbibed from that confounded low class thing the *Times* newspaper."

Curtis flourished his hand with a snap of the finger, and a silence very expressive; in another minute he stood at the entry port of the Flag Ship, opposite to which was lying the Saucebox steam frigate from England.

In a few minutes the captain's gig put off from the Saucebox, and pulled on board the Commander in Chief's ship.

The assembled middies at the entry port all fell back and made way for the captain, while the boatswain's mate gave the customary pipe of honor, and that dignified officer descended from one deck after another, until he finally gained the presence of the Commander in Chief.

The instant he was gone, the midshipman of his gig came running up the companion ladder of the Flag ship, and standing on her middle deck, the first question he put was—"Is Mr. Curtis on board?"

"Here am I," said Curtis.

"Here is a letter of introduction I have to you," said the midshipman, "and here is a whole heap of boxes and packages of all sorts for various officers of the Flag ship which my men will hand up from the boat."

"I am very much obliged to you," said Curtis, hastily breaking open his letter.

"My dear Scapegrace, will you come on board and dine with me to-day?"

"I should be very glad," said Scapegrace, who was our young friend of Portsmouth recollection—"but the fact is, I cannot come without asking the Skipper's leave, and our skipper has a little peculiarity."

"Peculiarity—what the dickens is his peculiarity?"

"Why, whatever favor you ask him he always has sixty excellent reasons for refusing it."

"Well, but zounds, you do not mean to say that he never grants any leave?"

"Well I do not mean to say anything of any kind or description when he is in the case, but I do not know of his ever having granted any leave."

"How the deuce do you get leave then?"

"Well, we always wait till he is out of the ship, and then ask the first lieutenant."

"Then how do the other officers get leave?"

"I believe they do the same."

"And how does the first Lieutenant get leave?"

"He waits until the Captain is out of the ship, and then he asks himself."

"Ah! capital, capital! What is the Skipper's name?"

"McCrotchet'"

"McCrotchet. Ah, a Scotchman, eh? What sort of order has he got your ship in?"

"Why he would tell you if you ask him, that she is a crack ship; but then, according to his own account, he always commanded the most crack ship of every station to which he belonged."

"Well, I am afraid you will have to wait some time before you get leave, if you have to wait till he goes on shore."

"Oh! we need not wait for that, you know, because very likely he will be coming on board the Admiral every day or so, or going somewhere else; and the moment he is over the ship's side, we all bustle up with our petitions to the first Lieutenant."

"What sort of a chap is your first Lieutenant?"

"Oh, he is a jolly fellow, and no mistake; but I have got a brother, a soldier officer, who is either out here or coming."

"What is his name?" said the assembled youngsters in chorus.

"Oh, his name, like mine, is Montagu."

"But yours is Scapegrace as well," they all cried with a laugh. "Why, in the name of glory did you take the name of Scapegrace?"

"For a capital good reason—any one of you young fellows would like that, or any other name, for the same reason. That excellent old Admiral Scapegrace left me thirty thousand pounds."

"Excellent indeed!" said Curtis: "I wish I had reasons for changing my name of the same sort, plenty as blackberries."

By this time Scapegrace and his new friend had reached the gun-room; and, in a trice, they produced before him all the dainties of the mess. These consisted chiefly of raisins, figs, &c., &c., a few potted meats, some excellent wine, and plenty of it.

"My eyes! Is not this a splendid pea coat," said the little youngster, dragging out a magnificent specimen of the marine watch coat.

"By jovey! have not I got a splendid pair of breeches?" said another, opening his packet in another quarter.

"I say, old Quiz-to-windward there, what are you reading all your sister's letter for over in that corner? What will you sell them for as soon as you have done with them?"

"Holloa, there; what have you got in that basket, you jolly old Cotton?" cried another.

"Cheese from my father—the Reverend old Parson at Cambridge."

"A cheese?" said one of his messmates; "why it is big enough to get in, and start to sea upon. A splendid fellow he is, Cotton. Now I vote we eat that cheese out carefully for you, and then pierce the wall, and ram it with 42-pounders; and if it would not batter down Fort Constantine, why you may call me ancient pistol."

"What has come out for you?" said one.

"What has come out for you?" said another.

"I have got a box of cigars," said a third.

And thus in the height of youthful delight, those favored youngsters, remembrances of whose friends had come to hand by her

Majesty's ship Saucebox, displayed and turned to one another their various treasures.

Ah! who can imagine half the pleasure and joy, when, in the midst of danger and peril, and far from home, these remembrances meet these longing, youthful, distant eyes, from the much-loved and absent hearth in some of those quiet country nooks of dear old England? Egad, it is almost worth undergoing the peril and misery of a sea life, to know the pleasure of such a moment.

"But I say, Mr. Curtis, you have not answered my question. Can you find out whether my brother has arrived?"

"What regiment is he in?"

"The Nonsuch."

"The Nonsuch! Why the Nonsuch has only just come out here a day or two ago."

"The Nonsuch; the Nonsuch came out in the Prince," said one of the midshipmen.

"No, they did not," said Curtis; "the Prince brought the 46th. The Nonsuch came out in some other transport; I forget her name."

"The Prince," said Scapegrace. "Is not that the magnificent large steamer that we saw lying close in shore at the entrance to Balaclava?"

"The same," said Curtis, "that is where she lies—she only came out early this morning."

"At any rate," said Scapegrace, "I will go on board the Prince and enquire."

"In either case, whoever she brought out, I think you will find that she landed all her troops, whether it was the Nonsuch, or whether it was the 46th."

"Well, I shall be going on shore immediately, I hope," said our friend, "and if she has landed her troops, whether it was the Nonsuch, or whether it was the 46th, whether they are landed or whether they are not, I can but call on my way to enquire, and having made sure of that, I can go on to the shore."

"But, my dear fellow," said Curtis, "if you can get leave to go on board the Prince, surely you can get leave to come here to dinner. Stay, though, I won't ask you, I forgot you have a brother here—you will be glad to see him of course. Come to-morrow and dine, though to-morrow you will not have had enough of your brother—come this day week and dine—Come."

"Well, I will if I can, you may be sure."

"Please, sir, I am sent down for the Saucebox's midshipman," said one of the quartermasters, presenting himself at the gun room door.

"Here am I," said Scapegrace starting up, "who wants me?"

"I beg your pardon, sir, it is your captain wants you on the quarter deck."

Julius hurried to the quarter deck, and here he found Captain McCrotchet.

"Mr. Scapegrace, take my gig on board," said the captain, "and tell the first Lieutenant to send her for me at four o'clock this afternoon."

"Aye, aye, sir," said Julius, turning away.

"Oh! and youngster," said the captain coming close up to him and stooping down, "tell my servant I dine with the Admiral, and to have everything ready for me to dress as soon as I come on board."

"Aye, aye, sir," replied the youngster and away he darted.

In a few minutes he was down over the Flag ship's side, in his boat, and rowing back to the Saucebox.

Julius had scarcely put off from the flag-ship, when there came right down upon her a squall of wind, that rattled through the rigging of the vast ship with a tremendous noise.

"Short stroke, my men," cried Montagu, "and feather your oars well—this is a sharp squall."

"Ah! sir, this is the sea for sharp squalls,"

said the old coxswain, bending to his oar as he spoke, and laying all his strength into it, while the gig scarcely made any perceptible way through the water, such was the fury of the breeze as it passed over the boat.

"Is it coming on to blow, Coxswain, do you think?" said Scapegrace, looking round him narrowly, and regarding the sky and water as if to make out what the coming weather was likely to be.

"Well, your honour, I don't know," said the coxswain: "this here Black Sea always was a treacherous place of business. I have sailed with many shipmates, who have traded over it, and been upon it a good deal in the course of their lives. I arn't been here much myself to be sure; but I am told it is very hard to know when it is going to blow and when it is not. Sometimes some of these squalls lengthen out into a regular gale of wind—sometimes they goes out just as they comes in, just like a lady's hystrikes. Does your honour know whether the glass has been falling?"

"No, Gasket: so far from falling, it has been rising."

"Ah! well, your honour, then perhaps I am mistaken; but, if the glass had not been rising, I should have said, there is as tight a gale of wind coming, as perhaps here and there one."

"Give way, my boys, give way," said the midshipman: "I declare, if the wind blows as hard as this, we shall be going astern in spite of our oars."

Again the men bent to the ashen blades till they curled and quivered under the force used, but for a long time they made little or no impression in the matter of speed.

After a few minutes' pulling, the fury of the wind began to moderate, and then the boat shooting ahead, pulled up under the larboard counter of the Saucebox, and Julius delivered his message to the first Lieutenant.

"Very well, Mr. Scapegrace," said the first Lieutenant, "Do you bear in mind then when four o'clock comes that you take the gig back to the captain."

"Aye, aye, sir," said Scapegrace; "please sir," said the youngster, who, as the reader will recollect, never wanted for what is vulgarly called impudence, but heroically called nerve—"would you be kind enough to let me pull in shore to that large transport, the Prince, and enquire for my brother, who has come out here in the Nonsuch Regiment?"

"Oh, is your brother in the Nonsuch?"

"Yes, sir, I believe he came out a day or two ago."

"Very well, you may pull in, and at the same time see what parcels and packets there are for the navy. As soon as the men have had their dinner, you may set off, but, remember, you will get into a scrape, you know, if you are not back at the Flag ship, as the bells strike four o'clock."

"I will be sure not to fail, sir, honour bright," said Julius.

The first Lieutenant smiled at the words "honour bright," and the captain's gig having been dropped astern the men came on board, and, with the midshipmen went to their various duties, for all hands had not yet been piped down from bringing the ship to.

"I will tell you what, master," said the first Lieutenant, "I do not at all like the weather here; I think I shall let go a second anchor underfoot, to be prepared for squalls."

"Ah! that you certainly had better," said the master, "and in addition to that I will see that the sheet anchor has its cable bent on all right and ready to let go. I do not at all like the spite that there is in that last gust of wind. It would not surprise me if it came on to blow great guns before midnight."

"Well, I do not know," said one of the lieutenants; "they say, you know, that in the

Euxine you get sharp gusts of squalls, but the wind never blows home."

"Ah!" said the master, "but there is a peculiar grunt which it gave. I wish I had as good a chance of going home this afternoon as we all have of hearing the wind blow home, this blessed night, if it holds on as it is going now. It is as squally as old mother Hubbard and her dog, when they had only a bone between them, and nothing to eat for a fortnight past. Did I hear you give that youngster leave to pull in shore to the Prince, Mr. Heathfield?"

"Yes," said the first Lieutenant, "he has a brother in the Nonsuch Regiment. He is a good, sharp youngster, and always willing and attentive and respectful and good tempered. He has to go back to the Skipper, on board the Flag Ship, at four, so I told him as soon as the men had finished their dinners, he might pull to the Prince and back."

"That may not be so easy," replied the master. "I very much doubt whether there will be any pulling betwixt this and the Prince this afternoon. The sea seems to be getting up in a way I do not understand if there is not more wind coming."

"Getting up, Master! why, hang it, you would get up too if you had half such a blast over your back as that poor sea had twenty minutes ago."

"Possibly so, but if that youngster is going to pull to the Prince you had better make him take one of the safety boat cutters. The wind comes down in such terrific puffs that a boat like the Captain's gig might be filled in a minute when one of those curling seas come bouncing into it."

"Yes, master, I think there is wisdom in that. Quarter-master run down for Mr. Scapegrace."

And down ran the Quarter-master for Mr. Scapegrace. In a few seconds up came that mercurial gentleman, all smiles and brilliancy.

"Youngster," said the first Lieutenant,

"the master thinks you cannot go to the Prince this afternoon."

"Does he, sir?" said the midshipman, looking a little sorrowfully at the master.

"Why, boy," said the Master, "I think it is coming on to blow very hard. I do not think you will be able to go without danger."

"O! if that is all, sir," said the boy, "the more the danger the more the fun."

"Yes, yes, you young monkey. It is fun enough drowning such a young cub as you, but where is the fun of damaging her Majesty's service by swamping half a dozen of the best seamen of the ship, as the Captain's gig's crew always is, or ought to be."

"Well, sir, if you think I ought not to ask it I will withdraw my request," said Scapegrace, turning to the first Lieutenant.

"No, my good boy, I never said so, and I do not think so. I was only trying you on, to see what you would say to it. If I thought there was any danger I would not let you go, but, as there are sudden squalls in this sea, and it is a long pull in shore to the Prince, instead of taking the Captain's gig, take the safety cutter, and then you know you can turn her over and over if you like the fun of danger, as it is only the month of November it will not do more than freeze your paws to cling to the thawts, and you can have as much danger as you desire. When you come back from the Prince, you can take the Captain's gig and go to the Flag ship, only mind you are on board here in time to do both, and caution the Captain's servant to be ready and not keep you waiting."

"Aye, aye, sir," said Scapegrace, and down he went to his berth to get his dinner.

END OF VOL. II.

CPSIA information can be obtained
at www.ICGtesting.com
Printed in the USA
LVHW040429110522
718423LV00002B/403

9 783375 001803